7/10

gimmeacall

sarahmlynowski

gimmeacall

DELACORTE PRESS

Copyright © 2010 by Sarah Mlynowski

All rights reserved. Published in the United States by Delacorte Press, an imprint of Random House Children's Books, a division of Random House, Inc., New York.

Delacorte Press is a registered trademark and the colophon is a trademark of Random House, Inc.

Visit us on the Web! www.randomhouse.com/teens
Educators and librarians, for a variety of teaching tools, visit us at www.randomhouse.com/teachers

Library of Congress Cataloging-in-Publication Data
Mlynowski, Sarah.
Gimme a call / Sarah Mlynowski. —1st ed.
p. cm.
Summary: After accidentally dropping her cell phone into a fountain at the mall, fourteen-year-old Devi Banks starts to get phone calls—and an earful of advice on how to live her life to avoid making disastrous choices—from her seventeen-year-old self.
ISBN 978-0-385-73588-9 (HC)—ISBN 978-0-385-90574-9 (GLB)
ISBN 978-0-375-89651-4 (e-book)
[1. Dating (Social customs)—Fiction. 2. Conduct of life—Fiction. 3. High schools—Fiction. 4. Schools—Fiction. 5. Telephone—Fiction.]
I. Title. II. Title: Give me a call.
PZ7.M7135Gi 2010
[Fic]—dc22
2009020020

The text of this book is set in 12-point Goudy.
Book design by Kenny Holcomb
Printed in the United States of America

10 9 8 7 6 5 4 3 2 1

First Edition

For Chloe, my little sweetheart

Acknowledgments

Thank you *thank you* **thank you** to:

Todd Swidler, my ever-patient, always-supportive,
extra-loving husband, who talked me through many,
many drafts of this book.

The people who made it happen: Wendy Loggia, my fabo editor;
Laura Dail, my incredible agent; and Tamar Rydzinski,
the queen of foreign rights.

All the awesome Random House Children's Books people:
Beverly Horowitz, Chip Gibson, Krista Vitola, Kelly Galvin,
Tamar Schwartz, Isabel Warren-Lynch, Kenny Holcomb,
Adrienne Waintraub, and Jennifer L. Black.

Richie Kern and the rest of the people at WME;
Andy Fickman and Betsy Sullenger at Oops Doughnuts Productions;
and the people at Paramount.

Aviva Mlynowski, who sang my praises to the
movie people—thank you, Squirt! Love you!

To my amazing early readers (I could not have done this without
your many insights . . . I was too pregnant and caffeine deficient):
Elissa Ambrose, my mom, who read the book as I wrote it;
Lauren Myracle, the master of praise and encouragement;
Lynda Curnyn, for her reading and commenting overnight;
Ally Carter, who reminded me to show instead of tell;
and Jess Braun, for showing me where to add depth.
Emily Jenkins, for telling me all the places to trim.

Targia Clarke, for her help with Chloe.

Love and thanks to my family and friends who kept me company while I wrote:
Larry Mlynowski, Louisa Weiss, John and Vickie Swidler, Robert Ambrose,
Jen Dalven, Gary Swidler, Darren Swidler, Shari Endleman, Emily Bender,
Heather Endleman, Shaun Sarno, Leslie Margolis, Alison Pace,
Bennett Madison, Cassandra Clare, Scott Westerfeld, Maureen Johnson,
Justine Larbalestier, Lauren McLaughlin, Robin Wasserman (and thank you,
Robin, for letting me interview you about Harvard!), Libba Bray,
Farrin Jacobs, Kristin Harmel, Bonnie Altro,
Jess Davidman, Laura Accurso, Avery Carmichael, and Bob.

gimmeacall

chapter one

Friday, May 23 • • • Senior Year

I should just return Bryan's watch to Nordstrom and go home. Instead, I'm sitting by the circular fountain in the Stonybrook Mall, staring at the window of the Sunrise Skin Spa. It features a poster of a wrinkle-free woman and the slogan *Go Back in Time*.

Sounds good to me. If I could go back in time, there's lots I'd tell my younger self. Including:

In third grade, do not let Karin Ferris cut your bangs. Your best friend is no stylist. She's going to accidentally cut them too short. And too crooked. And she won't always be your best friend either.

In fifth grade, do not put marshmallows in the toaster oven, even though it seems like a good idea. Toasty! Gooey! Yummy! No. When they expand, the tip of one of the marshmallows kisses the burner, and the toaster catches fire, and your entire family will forever bring up the story about how you almost burnt the house down.

Sophomore year: don't leave your retainer in a napkin in the cafeteria—unless you want to wade through three spaghetti-and-meatball-filled garbage bins to find it.

This December: do not buy the Dolly jeans you like in a size 4 because you believe they'll stretch. They will not.

May twenty-first: do not buy Him a silver watch for a surprise graduation present, because then you will spend senior skip day at the mall returning it. Which brings me to the most important tip.

About Him. Bryan.

If I could go back in time, the most important thing I would tell myself would be this: never *ever* fall for Bryan. I would warn fourteen-year-old me never even to go out with Him in the first place. Or even better—the party where we officially met when I was a freshman never would have happened. Okay, the party could have happened, but when he called me later and asked me out, I would have said no. Nice of you to ask but I am just not interested. Thanks but no thanks. Have a nice life. Maybe I'd tell myself to stay home instead and organize my closet.

Imagine that. Talking to my fourteen-year-old self. I wish.

I spot Veronica at Bella Boutique, right beside the Sunrise Skin Spa. She waves. I wave back. "Devi! Come see my new stock!" she calls. "It's stunning!" As if I'd listen to her. She's the one who swore up and down that my jeans would stretch. "I'll give you the employee discount!" she offers, even though I haven't worked a shift since the winter holidays.

"I'll come look in a minute," I call back to her. I rummage through my purse, find my phone, and dial for my messages. I want to hear the one he left this morning. Again. I've only listened to it once. Fine, seven times. I know: pathetic. But I keep hoping each time that it'll be different.

"Hi, Devi. It's me." Bryan's voice is low and raspy, like a smoker's. We tried cigarettes once, together, at the Morgan Lookout on Mount Woodrove when we were sophomores. But when we kissed, he tasted like a dirty sock, so that was the end of our smoking.

Until our relationship went up in smoke.

"I wish you'd answer," his voice continues. "You always answer." A pause as though he's waiting for me to answer. "I'm sorry. I mean, I'm really, really sorry. I never meant to hurt you."

The message is still playing in my ear, but I can barely hear, because now I'm crying, and my cheeks are all wet and my hand is all wet and how could he have told me he loves me when he obviously doesn't and—

Splash!

Like a bar of soap in the shower, my cell phone has slipped through my fingers and landed in the fountain.

Superb. One more thing to tell my younger (by two seconds) self: don't drop your cell phone into a house-size saucer of green chlorine. I peer into the water. A flash of silver twinkles up at me. Is that it? Nope. It's a nickel. The pond is filled with coins in addition to my phone. Are there really people out there who believe that throwing a nickel into the water can make a wish come true?

Aha! I see it, I see it! I stretch out to reach it, but it's a bit too far away. I lie down on my stomach and reach again. A little more . . . almost there . . .

The cell phone gets pulled further out of my reach by the swirling water jets within the fountain. Ah, crapola—I'm going to need to get in there.

Luckily, I'm wearing flip-flops. I look around to make sure no security people are watching, then stand on the bench, roll up the bottoms of my oxygen-depriving Dolly jeans, and step in.

Cold. Slimy. When I look down, my toes are bloated and tinted green. Maybe the water is radioactive and I'm turning into the Hulk.

Out of the corner of my eye, I spot Harry Travis and Kellerman marching through the mall like they own the place. Harry—definitely one of the best-looking guys in our class—has dark hair, a muscular build, intense blue eyes, and the rosiest skin. He also has this sexy stubble going on—very rugged and hot. And Kellerman—everyone just calls him Kellerman—looks like he's already part of a frat. He's always wearing his older brother's Pi Lambda Phi hat, and sweatpants.

I duck down so that the coolio senior duo won't see me. That would just make today perfect, wouldn't it? The water soaks through the knees of my jeans. Crap, crap, crap! When the guys turn in to the food court, I find my footing and try to relocate my phone. And there it is again! Yahoo! Balanced on top of a pyramid of nickels. Got it. Yes!

Now all I have to do is safely make it back to the side . . .

Splat. The swirls of water push me over, and the next thing I know, I'm flat on my butt. Great. Just great. My eyes start to prickle.

I heave myself up and back to the safety of the fountain's edge, leaving a trail of shiny green droplets. I ignore my sopping wet jeans—maybe the chemicals will help them stretch?—and wipe my phone against my shirt, as if that's gonna help. Please don't be broken, please, please, please. I press the power button.

No sound. No connection. No nothing.

I spot Veronica staring at me. "You okay?" she hollers.

Um, no? "I'm fine!" I wave, then turn back to the phone. I press power again. Still nothing. I press the one button. Nothing. The two. Nothing. Three, four, five, all nothing. Six, seven, eight, nine, the pound button, the volume button. Nothing, nothing, *nothing.* I kick the floor. My flip-flop makes a squishy sound.

I hit the power button. Again. Nothing.

I hit the nine, the eight, the seven, the six, the five, four, three, two, one, the pound button, the volume button. All nothing.

I press the send button. The phone comes alive.

There we go. I have no idea who I called, but it's ringing.

chapter two

Friday, September 9 • • • Freshman Year

The first time she calls, I'm sitting beside Karin Ferris and across from Joelle Caldwell and Tash Havens at our table in the cafeteria, the one in the back next to the garbage. Not ideal, since the location has a definite decaying-meat scent, but as far as I can tell, we're lucky to get any table. Some freshmen are sitting on the floor.

My two-week-old cell phone vibrates next to my half-eaten burnt grilled cheese and undercooked fries. Last week at orientation we were told that all us Florence West High School students—I'm finally a high school student! Crazy!—have to keep our cell phones on mute. There's so much vibrating going on in here, you'd think the cafeteria was built over a subway. It isn't, obviously. There is no underground transit in Florence, New York.

"Is that your sis?" Karin asks while slurping down a chocolate milk. "Tell her I say hi."

I get a quick glance at the Banks name on the caller ID and hit send.

"Hey, Maya!" I say, trying not to open my mouth too wide when I talk, as I suspect that a wedge of cheddar might be lodged between my two front braces. I hate these things. Yes, I have clear brackets, so it's not like I have a mouthful of metal, just a metal wire, but ever since I got them on last week, I've been constantly getting food stuck in there. Cereal, grilled cheese, undercooked fries—if it's on a plate, it's most definitely in my braces. "Hi!"

"Hello?"

"Finally! I've left you two messages this week! I know UCLA has a three-hour time difference, but I'm sure a smarty-pants like you can figure out how to get in touch," I tell her.

"Excuse me?" a girl says. A girl who isn't Maya. Huh? I look again at the caller ID but now it's blank.

Hmm. I have no clue who I'm talking to. But her voice sounds familiar, so maybe I should. It's like I'm watching a game show and I know the answer, I do, but it's on the tip of my tongue and I can't get it out. "Who is this?"

"Sorry, I think I called the wrong number," the girl says.

"No problem," I say, and hang up. I return to my grilled cheese.

"So what are you guys doing this weekend?" Karin asks.

"Nothing," Joelle says with a sigh. She adjusts her denim mini and off-the-shoulder blouse. "There is nothing to do. Maybe we should take a shopping road trip."

"To where? Buffalo?" Tash asks.

"Noooo, Buffalo is so lame. Let's go to Manhattan."

"Shall we take our flying bicycles?" Tash asks, rolling her massive and stunning green eyes. I don't know why she hides them behind glasses instead of wearing contacts. She hunches over when she sits too. I'd tell her to sit up straight and show off her height and supermodel's body, but I don't know her well enough yet.

"I wish we didn't live in the middle of nowhere," Joelle whines.

"You can't be bored two weeks into high school," Karin tells her.

"I can and I am," she says. "I'm thinking of joining yearbook. Anyone want to do it with me?"

None of us respond.

"You all suck." She sighs. "I have to find out if there are any parties this weekend. See where my future husband, Mr. Jerome Cohen, will be." She wiggles her pierced eyebrow.

I would definitely not mind going to a party with cute boys. I haven't had a boyfriend since Jarred Morgan, last year. We were together for four months. Before that was Anthony Flare. His name should have been warning enough. I should never have gone out with him. Karin liked him but she didn't tell me until after the two months we were together.

There are a few hotties in my classes. There's Harry Travis, who has gorgeous eyes, but doesn't hide them like Tash. His hair is dark, and he has the rosiest, softest-looking skin. He looks like he could play a TV heartthrob. And there's Joelle's Jerome Cohen, who's obviously off-limits, being Joelle's future husband, but still adorable in his low jeans and nineties band T-shirts. And there's this one guy I've noticed in the halls a few times, whose name I don't know. He doesn't usually stay in school for lunch, and I have no classes with him, but he has cute spiky hair and a big smile. I've never been on the receiving end of the smile, but I'm working on it.

My phone vibrates again. Another wrong number?

Joelle picks it up and squints at the caller ID. "You're calling yourself," she says.

I'm not sure what she means until I glance at the screen and see that it says my number. And my name. Now that's just weird. "Hello?" I say again.

"Oh, hi," the same girl as before says. "That's weird. I was trying to call my voice mail. I don't know why I keep getting you."

"Don't know why either," I say. I hang up again and take another bite of my sandwich.

The phone vibrates again.

Joelle leans over the table. "Who *is* it?"

I take another look at the caller ID. Still says my number. "Me again," I say. I take a quick sip of my apple juice, trying but failing to unstick the piece of cheddar in my teeth.

"There's something wrong with my phone," the familiar-yet-still-unidentified voice says. "I dialed my mom at work and I still got you. Can you tell me who I called?"

"Devorah Banks," I answer in my polite voice, the one I use with teachers, new people, and dogs. I don't know why

I use it with dogs. It might be because the very sight of their big mouths and sharp vampire teeth makes me break out in hives and I hope they'll interpret my courteous tone as a peace offering.

"Oh, good, you know me," she says.

"I do?" I ask.

"Well . . . you just said my name."

I press the phone hard against my ear to try to block out the chaotic noise of the caf. Am I missing something? "What are you talking about?"

"Who is this?" she asks again.

"This is Devorah Ba—" I stop in midname. Why am I giving out personal info to a stranger on the phone? "Sorry, but who is *this*?"

"Look," she barks. "My jeans are sopping in green goo and I'm having a really bad day. Can you please just tell me who I'm talking to?"

"Um . . . ," I say, and then giggle.

I giggle a lot. When I'm nervous, when I'm happy, when I'm around boys, when I'm sitting in class. Seriously. On Monday, I was at Karin's house and I pressed play on her tape recorder. She tapes all her classes, including American history (one of the two classes I have with her)—she's kind of a perfectionist that way—and the next thing I heard was my giggling reverberating around her bedroom. Like a hyena. He-he-he-he-he-he. So awful. Giggling, in American history! There's nothing funny about Ms. Fungas's history class. Except her name, which is downright hilarious. Fungas! Tee-hee. There I go again.

"Obviously you know me. You just said my name," the girl on the phone snaps. "Are you going to tell me who you are?"

Er. Is this some kind of scam? A telemarketer trying to get my information so she can steal my identity and charge a Thanksgiving trip to Panama on a fake credit card? If only I had a credit card. Maybe I should steal my own identity. Instead, I ask, "Would you like to tell me what number you're trying to call?"

"I tried to call my mom's number at work! And before that I tried to call my voice mail! And before that I just hit the send button!" she says, her pitch rising. "But each time, the display just has these weird symbols on it!"

"Well, you called me," I say, starting to get annoyed.

Joelle waves at me from across the table. "Do you know who it is yet?"

I shrug. "No idea."

"Then hang up," she orders. "You're wasting your minutes."

"I think it's a prank," I whisper back. I take another sip of juice to clear my braces.

"Want me to tell him to get lost?" Joelle asks.

"Her," I say, correcting her, and reach across the table to hand her the phone. If someone wants to take control of the situation, I'm happy to let 'em.

"Watch the—" Tash warns, but her voice is too soft and I hardly hear her.

"What?"

"I said watch the . . . French fries."

Too late. I've just dragged my beige sleeve directly through the ketchup-soaked fries.

I jerk my arm and the phone back toward me . . . and right into my Snapple bottle. The bottle teeters—don't spill, don't spill!—then decides to go for it. It tips over, and gushes down the table.

"Whoops!" Fantastic. Must not try to do multiple things at once. Talking on the phone while checking e-mail? I end up typing my conversation. That game in which you try to pat your head with one hand, rub your stomach with the other, click your tongue, and make the *uhhh* sound at the same time? If I tried it, I'd end up in the emergency room in a pretzel position.

"Sorry! I gotta go," I tell the stranger.

I hang up and sprint toward the lunch line in search of napkins.

The phone vibrates inside my backpack when I'm leaving school for the day. I dig around, but my cell has somehow ended up at the bottom of the bag, buried under seven hundred loose pieces of paper, my French conjugation book, *Jane Eyre*, and my American history binder.

"Ready?" Karin asks me. She's waiting for me at the front door.

The phone vibrates again. I scrape my hand on a pencil but finally find it. Maya? I glance at the caller ID.

It says my number. My number is calling me *again*. What is going on? "Hello?"

"It's you," the girl from before says. "Good. I must have misunderstood you earlier. When you said, 'This is Devorah Banks,' you meant *me*, right? As in I'm Devorah Banks? You recognized my voice?"

What is she talking about? "This is Devorah," I say slowly. "Me. *I'm* Devorah. Who are you?"

"This is Devorah Banks!" she screams. "I am Devorah Banks! Just tell me who this is!"

Hotness erupts at the base of my neck and spreads to my cheeks like a bad rash. "I'm. Devorah. Banks."

"You can't be," she says. "That's impossible! I'm hanging up!" The phone goes dead. A second later, it vibrates. Again, my number.

"Still me," I sing.

"You're crazy!" she screams.

"Alrighty then." I press end, turn off the power, and toss the phone back into my bag. What, am I going to stay on the phone with some nut job who calls me names? I don't think so. There's a tingling on the back of my neck, and I try to scratch it away. I hurry to catch up with Karin. "Sorry."

The mid-September air cools me down like a glass of ice water. Or like wet cotton, which is what I've been wearing since lunch, when I tried, unsuccessfully, to rinse the ketchup out of my shirt.

We spot a pack of students playing softball on the baseball diamond and pause outside the wire fence to watch.

"Tryouts," Karin says, pointing to the scoreboard. "Baseball, basketball, and soccer today; cheerleading, swim, and gymnastics on Monday. I'm so nervous."

"Don't be. You're definitely going to make the gymnastics team."

"Maybe. Maybe not." She twirls a blond ringlet between her fingers.

"Oh, please. You're a shoo-in. You've been doing gymnastics since you were six. You're gonna make it."

"You should try out for something too," she tells me.

"Sure," I say. "Maybe cheerleading."

"I can see that," she says seriously.

I burst out laughing. "Oh, shut up, you cannot. I'm the most inflexible person in the history of the world. And I can't dance and sing at the same time. Plus I'm too short. Those girls are all gazelles. You be the athlete. I'll be the . . ." My voice trails off. I don't know what I'll be. "Why don't *you* try out for cheerleading?"

"Yeah, right," she says.

"Why not?" I ask.

"First of all, I don't think you can be on both the gymnastics team and the squad. Travel conflicts. And second, I'm not pretty enough to be a cheerleader."

I flick her on the arm. "You are so!"

"Am not." She shakes her ringlets.

Karin will never admit she's pretty—even though she is. She'll say, "My nose is too wide and crooked," or "My eyes are too far apart," or "I have no boobs," even though her nose is fine, her eyes are normally spaced, and a 34B is *not* nothing. I'm a 34B, thank you very much.

"You are so," I tell her.

"Well, so are you," she says.

"Of course I am," I say with an overdramatic toss of my hair. Then I giggle. It's not that I think I'm gorgeous or anything, but I'm not insecure about it. Sure, I break out on my nose and forehead, but whatever. Who doesn't? I'm fine with my looks. Or I will be after I get my braces off. I point to the fence. "Wanna watch?" Maybe watching cute boys will cheer her up. It usually cheers me up.

"For a sec. But then my mom's taking me to the mall. I need some new sneakers. Wanna come? We'll treat you to a Cinnabon."

It's not like I'm going to hang out here by myself. "Sure."

Karin points to Celia King, who's sitting on the bleachers. "Joelle got us all invited to her party tonight."

"Seriously?" I ask, impressed.

"Yup."

"Celia's so sparkly," I say. "It's like she bathes in glitter."

"Switch it up!" the referee on the field screams, and everyone in the outfield runs in. A crew of new guys take their places.

Karin holds on to the fence and leans back. "So do you want to go to the party?"

"Obviously," I say. "It's a good thing your parents are friends with Joelle's parents. 'Cause she's certainly connected."

"Yeah. She knows people from all the different middle

schools. And I know she can be a bit bossy, but she means well."

"I like her," I say. "I like Tash too. I thought she was snobby at first, but I think she's just shy."

"I know. It's because she's so gorgeous. With a little styling—"

"Don't you dare. I'm going to tell her what you did to my bangs."

"That was in the third grade."

"You're lucky I forgave you."

Karin grins. "I'll keep my hands to myself. Promise. You know, Tash is supposedly a science genius."

"Seriously? I have chemistry with her. She hasn't said much yet."

"I'd pick her as my lab partner if I were you. Joelle told me that her mom died of leukemia back in elementary school and now her goal is to be an oncologist when she grows up so she can cure cancer."

"That's . . . so sad," I say. I'm impressed that she has a goal. Better than my goal, which is to meet cute boys and avoid getting cheese stuck in my braces.

"So tonight," Karin continues, "we're meeting at Tash's at eight and then we'll walk over. Celia lives in Mount Woodrove."

"Fancy." Mount Woodrove is one of the most expensive areas in town.

We watch as a goateed, giant junior at bat whacks the ball and sends it flying into the outfield. And wait! The cute, spiky-haired guy with the fabo smile who I've noticed in the hallways chases after it. Now he's wearing a black and red baseball jersey and running backward to catch the ball, his glove above his head.

He's got it, he's got it, he's got it—he jumps and tries to catch it—he don't got it.

The ball sails way over his spiky hair. Miles over. Like me, he's on the wrong side of five foot five, and when he jumps, he somehow falls backward and lands on his butt. Ow. Spiky immediately springs to his feet, takes off after the ball, grabs it, and shoots it to second base, but it's way too late.

"Safe!" the referee yells.

Spiky shakes his head in defeat, but he's smiling. A big, broad, two-dimpled liquefy-my-heart kind of smile.

"You okay?" Jerome Cohen, the third baseman, asks him. Instead of a jersey, he's wearing an old Foo Fighters T-shirt and ripped jeans.

Spiky salutes him. "I've been working on that move all week."

Cohen laughs.

"Do you know who that is?" I ask Karin. His track pants are covered with dirt, his jersey completely disheveled, but his cheeks are red and he's laughing.

"Jerome Cohen," she says. "That's the guy Joelle has a crush on."

"No, I know *that* guy. He's in my algebra class. I mean the guy who dropped the ball."

"Ryan. He went to Carter. No—sorry, it's Bryan. Bryan Sanderson."

Hello, Bryan Sanderson.

chapter three

Friday, May 23 • • • Senior Year

After my sucky day at the mall, I dump my broken cell phone onto my nightstand, leave my stupidly uncomfy and now bleach-scented jeans in a heap on my floor, wash green goo off my legs in the tub, and roll on a pair of sweatpants. Then I pop by my father's home office to check in. "Hey, Dad."

He's sitting in his brown bathrobe. His slippered feet are up on the desk. They're Mickey Mouse slippers. We went to Disney when I was seven. Not that I remember the last real family vacation we went on, but I've seen the pic on the living room mantel. "Hi, hon," he says, scratching the back of his mostly gray head. "How was senior skip day?"

Would have been better if I'd had someone to skip with. "Boring. How was your day?"

"Fine."

He doesn't look fine. He looks like he could use some color. And a trip to the gym. An empty pizza box is sitting on his desk. "When will Mom be back?"

"Later," he says, not looking up.

"Any job leads?" I ask, peeking at the chessboard on his computer screen.

"Not today."

I return to my room, close my door, and decide that it's time to toss all things Bryan, starting with the framed pictures we took with the now broken camera I bought for him. I'll dump them into my garbage pail one at a time like I'm performing an exorcism. They're cheap plastic frames anyway. I take a deep breath. Here goes. Bryan and me out for Chinese for his fifteenth birthday. Dump. Bryan and me on the Ferris wheel at the Florence carnival. Dump. Me sitting on Bryan's lap on my sixteenth birthday. Dump. Bryan on a swing. Dump. Bryan and me the day I got my braces off. My bright white teeth are practically the entire picture. Bryan and me dressed up as vampires for Halloween. That was just seven months ago. We weren't going to dress up, but then we saw these ridiculous fangs at the drugstore, and voilà! We covered our faces in white makeup, drove to his cousins' house, and offered to take them trick-or-treating. They ate too many SweeTarts and threw up in the back of Bryan's blue Jetta.

Maybe I'll leave this one up for now, since it reminds me of vomit.

Bryan has copies of all these pictures too. I put them in a scrapbook for him for his birthday. It was a gorgeous scrapbook. There was calligraphy involved. I had way too much fun making it. Waste of time. It's probably in his trash now.

What else has Bryan given me?

My TV. He gave it to me when his father and stepmom, not realizing that his mom had gotten him a TV the year before, sent him one as a birthday gift. It's not like I want to get rid of that.

I fiddle with the bracelet he bought me for our one-year anniversary. Its five white-gold hearts are strung together on a delicate white-gold chain. I can't toss jewelry, can I? Maybe I should sell it. I should at least take it off. I fiddle with the lobster-claw clasp but it won't budge. Fantastic. I need a girlfriend to do this for me. I need to go to a girlfriend's house or get her to take me shopping or come over and watch sad movies with me, but . . . I don't have any girlfriends. Pathetic, no?

I used to have girlfriends, but not anymore. I've spoken to no one all day except my former boss and my dad. Oh, and an obnoxious younger girl who thinks she's me.

Why would someone claim to be me? My life sucks. Unless her name really is Devorah Banks. Maybe there's another one. And somehow when I dropped the phone into the fountain, our lines got crossed. Yes. That must be it. I sit down at my computer and search for my own name online. There are 105 hits. Doctor Devorah Banks! Lawyer Devorah Banks! Who knew? So my line just got crossed with another Devorah Banks. There ya go. Problem solved. I push my computer chair away from my desk.

The back of my neck begins to tingle. Kind of a coincidence that my line would get crossed with another Devorah Banks's, though, no? And here's the strange thing: the girl on the other end of the line, she did sound kind of familiar.

She sounded like me.

Hah! As if. Maybe dropping my cell phone into the fountain was like tossing in a penny. And didn't I wish to talk to my fourteen-year-old self?

I swivel my chair back and forth. Hah. You can't drop your cell phone into a fountain and then call your younger self. That's ridiculous.

I grab the cell, stare at it suspiciously. Then hit the send button. It rings and then goes to voice mail. My voice mail?

"Hiya, this is Devi. I'm out and about and can't take your call. Sorry! Leave me your deets and I'll get back to you as soon as I have a sec. Bya!"

Beep.

Is someone messing with me? Someone must be messing with me. Even the voice on the message sounds like mine. But it is not the message I have on my phone. My message is a recording of Bart Simpson saying that I can't come to the phone, and not to have a cow.

Bryan loves *The Simpsons*.

Maybe someone hacked into my phone and rerecorded my message?

A chill spreads up my back. Wait. I made that message. On my cell phone. When I was a freshman.

Sure, it sounds like a simple message to record, no? But it wasn't. It took five takes before I didn't sound like a giggling freak. Okay, eight takes.

I made Karin call it. "It's fabo," she said. Everything was fabo back then.

It can't be my freshman message. Why would my freshman message still be on my phone?

I jump out of my seat. I need a snack. My brain is obviously malnourished. I hurry to the kitchen and rummage through the fridge. Half-empty carton of milk. Processed cheese slices. Apples that have seen better days. No wonder my dad has pizza places on speed dial. I find a warm can of Coke and a slightly stale box of Froot Loops in the cupboard and spread myself across the graying living room couch.

As I crunch on my cereal, I figure out the answer to the phone issue. The phone must have deleted my recorded message when it fell into the water. And . . . and it's replaying the one I left when I first bought it.

Hmmm. My theory explains the message, but how does it account for the girl who keeps answering the phone and saying she's me?

Hah—maybe I did just call my freshman self by accident. Yeah, right. Not possible.

My neck begins to tingle again. What is up with that?

Maybe I'm not such a good judge about what's possible

and what's not. I never thought it possible that Bryan and I would break up.

So who knows what's possible? Maybe I *did* make a wish. Maybe it *did* come true. Maybe I did call myself in the past. Maybe I can keep calling myself in the past. I take another gulp of Coke. Maybe I'm losing my mind.

chapter four

Friday, September 9 • • • Freshman Year

I'm in the kitchen with Mom, telling her about my day. She's rummaging through the fridge for ingredients while I set the table. She's making her lemon chicken, my favorite.

"How was chemistry?" she asks. "Did you get lost again?"

"Not terribly." The corridors in my new school are like a maze, but she's not talking about my finding my way. I reach into the cupboard for three plates.

"Only two," Mom says, splaying three chicken breasts onto the cutting board. "Dad's stuck at the office. I'll warm his food up for him later."

Shocker. I put one of the plates back.

"I was never good at science," she continues. "Maybe Dad can help you."

"If he's ever home, maybe," I mutter.

She sighs. "Don't start. It's a busy time for him at work."

"The last five years have been a busy time," I say. "Whatever. You never get mad at him."

"Yes I do," she says. "Did you see the picture I finally printed out from our anniversary dinner? I put it on the mantel."

I drop the napkin I'm folding and check out the eight-by-ten glossy photo in the shiny silver frame beside the Disney photo and a bunch of photos of me and Maya. Me and Maya all sudsy in the bath. Me and Maya wearing matching purple polka-dot dresses. Me and Maya hugging and stuffed into one of my dad's woolly sweaters. In the anniversary shot, Dad is looking a little pale and scrawny, but Mom is looking fabo in a low-cut black dress. I hope I look as good as she does when I'm her age. She can still fit into my clothes. "Very foxy," I tell her.

Mom stretches out a piece of chicken on her cutting board and slices off a hunk of fat. "So, how was the mall?" she asks. "Did you get anything?"

"A new nail polish. Plum. Nice, huh?" I lift it out of its bag to show her. "And what did *you* do today?"

Slice, slice. "Did Karin find shoes?"

"She did. You know, Mom, there was a career fair at the mall today near the food court. There were all these pharmaceutical booths and cosmetic company booths and telemarketing booths. I was thinking you should go by this weekend to see if there's anything you want to do."

"Do you want me to make you a snack?" she asks, ignoring me.

"I'll find myself something," I tell her, and open the pantry.

"No marshmallows," she jokes.

"Ha-ha. Do we have any Froot Loops?"

"Why don't you have some grapes? I just washed them."

I open the fridge and pull out a bowl of purple grapes plucked off the stem. Someone has way too much time on her hands.

"Back to you getting a job—"

She laughs again. "Devi, I don't have time to get a job."

"Yes, you do. I get that you wanted to stay home with us when we were little, but now it's only me and I pretty much take care of myself. Dad is never here, so he doesn't need too much looking after either. You need a job. Or at least some hobbies. Why not go by?"

"Because I don't want to be a telemarketer," she says tightly. "And I have a hobby. I cook."

"Besides cooking," I say. I plop down onto the kitchen chair and take out my new nail polish.

My cell phone rings. I put down the still unopened bottle of polish and look at the caller ID. Her. Again.

"You are not going to apply nail polish while you're sitting at our new wood table, are you?" Mom asks.

Busted. "Um . . ."

"Why don't you cut up some Gruyère to go with the grapes?"

The phone rings again.

"Because the cheese slicer's a weapon. Do you know

how many times I've cut my thumb on it?" The phone rings a third time.

"Why aren't you answering?" Mom asks.

I have to tell Crazy Stalker Girl to quit bugging me. "Yes," I answer.

"Devi," the girl says. "Don't hang up!"

"Hold on," I tell her. I grab my bottle of polish, hurry up to my room, and close the door. "What do you want?"

"I'm confused," she says. "And I'm hoping you can explain it to me. The message on your voice mail—your outgoing message—that was *my* message!"

"Huh?" Crazy Grumpy Stalker Girl makes no sense. I sit down at my desk, lean the cell between my ear and shoulder, open my new bottle of polish, and spread out my left hand.

"The one you left on your voice mail! 'Hiya, this is Devi'!" She raises the pitch of her voice, I guess in an effort to sound like me. Although—*okay, s-t-r-a-n-g-e*—she kinda already does sound like me. "That was my message!"

What? "You have the same message on your voice mail?"

"I did. Three and a half years ago."

"Uh . . . okay." My neck starts to tingle. I ignore it and apply the plum polish to my pinky nail.

"You have to tell me the truth," she insists. "Are you really Devi Banks?"

"*Yes.*"

"And you're a freshman?"

"Yes." Next finger.

"At Florence West?"

"Yes." For the last two weeks, anyway. Not that I'm giving this weirdo any additional info. My stomach is kind of jittery. The girl is nuts. Incredibly nuts.

"This is insane," she says. "Incredibly insane."

Now my hand is tingling. "Can I go now?" I mumble. I just dripped polish down my finger. Crazy Girl is ruining my concentration.

"No! What time is it there? Seven?"

I carefully turn my neck to glance at the alarm clock without dropping the balancing phone. "Yes. Seven-oh-four."

"Here too. This is so wild! And what time was it when I first called you today?"

"Um, lunchtime?"

"It was today, right?"

This is too much. "Alrighty. I gotta go."

"No! Wait! Okay, I know I sound psycho. But . . . Devi?"

"Yes," I say. Psycho? The girl is certifiable. "That is still my name."

"Right. See, I was at the mall and I dropped my phone into the fountain. And I had been thinking about all the things I would tell myself in the past. And now I'm talking to you."

"What," I say slowly, "are you talking about?" I would hang up, should hang up, but she sounds so familiar.

"Don't you see?" she says, sounding like she's bursting with excitement. "I'm pretty sure I'm you. In the future."

chapter five

Friday, May 23 ● ● ● Senior Year

How strange is this?

I jump out of my bed and start pacing up and down my carpet. "Freshman Me? You there?" Why isn't she saying anything? "I know—we need to test this out," I say. "Maybe you should rip down some of the wallpaper or something, so I can see it. Or leave me a note. I could be wrong about this, obviously, but I don't think I am."

No response.

"Hello?" I say.

"Shoot," she says. "I spilled my nail polish all over the carpet."

"You did?" I ask. My heart leaps. "Where?"

"Near my desk," she sighs. "My mom is going to kill me."

I drop to my knees and examine the area around the desk legs. Oh. My. God. There is an hourglass-shaped brownish stain on the carpet! A stain that was not there before! She's really me! "I see it!" I scream. "I see the stain! You spilled nail polish and I see it!" That so wasn't there five minutes ago! It's her! It's really her! I mean it's me! It's really me! My brain is whirling. Not only did I call myself in the past, but if I can see the spilled polish, then changing her present affects *my* present. "Do you know what this means?"

Silence.

"Hello?" I ask. "You still there?"

"Still here," she says.

"You believe me, right?"

"Of course I do," she says. "So, what am I like in the future? Do cars fly?"

"I'm so glad you believe me!" I exclaim. "I wasn't sure how you—I mean, I—were going to react. I mean, I know it's tough to believe, but what other explanation could there be? You have to admit it, our voices sound exactly alike, no? Well, not exactly, since mine's more mature, but close enough. I mean, if I can believe something like this, so can you, since you *are* me. Yay! But to answer your question, cars don't fly. It's only been a few years. I'm only a senior. Tell me, what day is it today over there?"

"It's Friday, September ninth," she squeaks.

"Seriously? That's so wild. September ninth freshman year?"

"Um, yup."

Talk about *Freaky Friday*. "It's Friday here too. End of May."

"Of course it is!" she says in a super-chipper voice. "Where is here again?"

It must be confusing for her too. "Four years later! Actually, three years, eight months. I'm a senior."

"Right-o."

"Hmmm, I wonder why I got you on Friday, September . . ." My hands feel cold. I can't believe this is happening. I know what today is for her. "It's Celia's party tonight, isn't it?"

She pauses. "You know Celia?"

"Of course I do! I still go to school with her. Unfortunately. So it's her party tonight, right? Isn't it?"

"It . . . is."

Oh. My. God. I know how to *really* test this. I know what I have to do. I'm going to change the past. I'm going to fix everything. "Okay, listen to me," I say carefully, sitting down on my computer chair. "Don't go." I have a plan. For the first time in four years, I have a *plan*. A brilliant one!

"Excuse me?"

"Don't go," I repeat. "Stay home. Watch TV. No— organize your closet! You're going to change everything for us!"

"Sure. No problem. I have to go," she says. "My call-waiting is beeping."

Huh? We're having an important conversation here! Why would she possibly want to take another call? What could be a better call than one from your future self? "Who is it?" I ask incredulously.

"My sister," she says.

"Maya?" I ask. "Seriously?"

"How do you know my sister's name?"

I laugh. Maya is calling! A younger Maya, of course. It must be a younger Maya, because the last time I looked forward to talking to Maya was probably three and a half years ago. All right, that's not entirely true, but it feels like that. ".Okay, go talk to her," I say, "while you still can. I'll call you later."

Freshman Me doesn't respond, but that's okay. She's absorbing. As soon as it soaks in, though, she's going to have a lot of questions.

Which is good, because I have all the answers.

About an hour after I get off the phone with Freshman Me, my mom knocks on my door, then opens it. "How're you doing?" she asks, all concerned. She's still in her work outfit—black pants and a white blouse. The top button of her pants is already unbuttoned. It's the first thing she does when she gets home. That and eat my dad's left-over pizza. We used to share clothes, but those days are long gone.

I'm obviously not going to tell her about my magical cell phone. She'd just think the breakup has tossed me off the deep end.

I open my closet and pretend to be rifling through it. "I'm kind of busy," I tell her.

She sighs. "Well, if you want to talk, I'll be in the living room." Translation: she's going to plant herself on the couch and watch the Food Network, like always.

About ten minutes later, the house line rings, and I hear my mom pick up. Then she yells upstairs: "Devi! Phone!"

My heart stops. For me? My cell isn't working. . . . Could it be . . .

"Who is it?" I ask, standing up.

"Maya!"

Oh. Maya. Mom must have told her about Bryan. I'm sure Maya will try to rub it in now—she was right, my whole life shouldn't be about Bryan, blah, blah, blah. I pick up the house extension in my room. "Hey."

"I just heard the news," she says. "I just wanted to tell you that it's probably for the best."

I roll my eyes. "Thanks, Maya. That's just what I need to hear."

"No, I'm serious, Dev. It's about time you're on your own. You're way too young to be so serious with some guy."

Well, no worries, Maya. In a few minutes, the whole dating-Bryan thing will never have happened. Because of my brilliant plan.

"You need to explore your options," Maya continues.

"Didn't realize you were the dating expert," I say a little bit meanly.

"I'm not saying I'm an expert. I'm just saying—"

"What?"

"Never mind. If you're going to yell at me, can you put Mom back on the phone?"

"I'm not yelling," I say extra calmly.

There's a long pause. When did it get so weird between us, anyway?

"So, are you packing up?" I ask, trying to change the subject. "Excited to travel?"

"I am excited. Nervous about law school, but psyched to have some time to roam. What are you doing this summer? Now that you're not with Bryan, want to come backpack Europe with me?"

Am I hallucinating, or does her voice lose a little of its certainty when she asks that? She couldn't be nervous about asking me . . . could she?

Of course not. She's probably not even serious.

"Yeah, right," I say. "As if Mom and Dad would let me backpack."

"They'd let you come with me. Maybe not for the whole summer, but for a few weeks. You could meet me in Italy. Check out the real Florence."

Imagine, Maya and me traveling by train across Europe, staying up late in youth hostels, making up songs and singing at the top of our lungs in foreign countries . . . although she'd probably end up lecturing me half the time. Flirting with too many boys, not caring enough about the museums, etc., etc. "I don't know." A few weeks alone with my sister? We'd probably want to strangle each other. "I was planning on . . ." Hanging out with Bryan. Occasional shifts at Bella. "Working."

"Are you saving up to try to move into a dorm?"

"We were—" I stop in midsentence. Bryan and I talked about maybe one day getting a place off campus. "Maybe," I say instead.

"You would love the dorm," she says. "I had so much fun my first year of college."

"Yeah, well, I don't know how great the dorms are at Stulen."

"You could always transfer. You can put a little more effort into your grades now that Bryan isn't around."

"Thanks, Mom," I say. Not that my mom ever bugs me about my grades. Nope. Only Maya. I close my eyes. "Listen, I have to go." I don't want to spend the next hour being lectured about all the ways I'm screwing up my future. Especially since I'm fixing it all on my own. With my brilliant plan.

"Okay. Just try not to obsess about Bryan breaking up with you."

"I won't," I promise. Because as long as Freshman Me doesn't go to Celia's party, I'll be breaking up with him first.

chapter six

"Smile!" Joelle orders, holding out the camera and cramming me, Tash, Karin, and herself into the frame. "Okay, let's go," she says after the flash goes off. She strides toward the front door of Celia's ginormous house.

"Wait!" Karin cries, grabbing my arm. "Is my makeup okay?"

"Perfect," I tell her. "How's mine?"

"Fabo. My mom's lipstick looks gorge on you."

I give her a big fake smile. "Does it make my braces more or less obvious?"

"Less. Definitely. How's my breath?" She exhales.

"Minty. Mine?" I breathe out.

"Like a fresh fall day."

"Are you guys always such freaks before parties?" Tash

asks, adjusting her glasses. She's wearing the same thing she wore to school today—jeans and a black shirt.

"Yup," we both answer, clinging to each other's arms. It's our pre-party ritual.

Joelle pushes her shoulders back, strikes an I'm-hot-stuff pose in her red minidress, and rings the doorbell. I'm not the biggest fan of red. But Joelle makes it work.

"Would you like a breath test?" Karin asks Tash as we huddle outside the door.

"I'll pass," she says.

When no one answers, Joelle turns the doorknob. It opens onto a marble entranceway packed with Florence West students—some of whom I recognize, most of whom I don't. Harry Travis is standing with Kellerman and Sean Puttin by the stairs. Harry's eyes are extra blue and his cheeks are extra rosy. Definitely hot. Sean flicks up his collar. He's super preppy—always looks like he's about to play tennis. And Kellerman might be the only guy in the room wearing sweatpants instead of jeans.

I peer around the room, wondering if Bryan's here.

"Joelle, Tash, hi," Celia says, gliding toward us in low jeans and a strapless black top. "Joelle, you look like you're here for a Christmas party. Adorable. And, Tash! I'm so glad you're here. My parents keep their booze above the fridge and no one here is tall enough to reach."

"Hi, Celia," Tash says dryly. "Do you know Karin and Devi?"

Her forehead crinkles. "Debbie?"

"Devi," I say.

"That's a name?"

"It's short for Devorah," I explain, feeling my cheeks burn.

"Adorable," she says, twirling and sparkling. She's definitely wearing glitter on her shoulders. Next she turns to Karin. "You have adorable hair. I bet it would look amazing if you blew it straight."

"Oh, um . . . thanks?" Karin responds uncertainly.

Celia blows us a kiss and disappears into the living room.

"Is my hair too curly?" Karin whispers to me, her brows furrowed.

"Ignore her," Tash says, and closes the door behind us. The lights are low, the R & B is blasting, and I'm pretty sure it's at least a hundred degrees in here. I slip off my sweater and cram it into my purse. I hope that in all this evening's craziness, I remembered to put on deodorant.

I wasn't even sure if I should come to the party after the prank call I got.

What kind of horrible, obnoxious person calls another girl and tells her to stay home and organize her closet instead of going to a party?

Maya convinced me to come anyway.

"It's probably someone who wasn't invited to the party and doesn't want to be the only person stuck at home,"

Maya insisted during our call. "Ignore. Go. Stop answering your phone."

So here I am. I always listen to Maya. She *is* the smart one. I'm the pretty one. She takes after my dad, I take after my mom. Not that I'm pretty by a Florence West standard. Just a Banks standard.

Maya hates when I call her the smart one. "You're just as smart as I am," she always tells me. "You just need to focus on school instead of only boys."

I miss having her in the next room giving me constant advice. During our quick pre-party phone call, my stomach ached at the sound of her voice. "When are you coming home for a weekend?" I asked.

"Already? I just got here!"

"But I miss you! It's not like Mom or Dad will make up new words to songs and sing them with me in the backyard at the top of their lungs."

"So visit me. Wanna come for Columbus Day weekend? Supposedly the dorm throws crazy parties. Lots of cute boys," she added, laughing.

"Yes!" I hollered.

"We'll look for tickets," she promised, before saying she had to get off to get ready for a dorm party.

I hoped she'd stake out a cute boy for herself. Last year, I peeked at her diary—she should not have left it under her mattress if she didn't expect me to read it—and I discovered that she had never kissed a boy on the lips.

While I had already kissed two boys on the lips.

Maybe Maya will find a boyfriend at her party.

I follow Tash into the living room.

Maybe I'll find a boyfriend at *this* party.

I'm sitting on Celia's couch, minding my own business, laughing, giggling, whatever, about to deposit a tortilla with a dab of salsa into my mouth when I hear "Hey, Sands!"

Bryan Sanderson, the spiky-haired, passionate yet average baseball player with the fabo smile, is standing in the doorway to the living room. He's wearing faded jeans and a soft-blue T-shirt layered over a long-sleeved gray one.

As my stomach does a little jumping jack, my chip somehow frees itself from my fingers, flies through my legs, and lands on Celia's living room sectional.

Celia's white suede sectional.

Splat! Omigod. Why would someone with a white suede sectional serve salsa? If I had a white suede sectional, I'd serve only white party foods, like french onion dip and cauliflower. Better yet, marshmallows. Is serving salsa not asking for trouble? Why would a couch be white, anyway? What if you have dirt on your jeans? Or an open pen in your pocket? What then?

No, no, no. I mustn't blame the victim, aka the couch, for my inability to eat and spot a cute guy at the same time.

What do I do, what do I do?

I slam my legs together while keeping them elevated—

to avoid smearing the stain—and debate my next move. Jump up and try to clean the couch? Act clueless? Confess to Celia?

Deep breath. *Deeeeeeep breeeaaaaath*. First I must assess the damage. Perhaps I imagined the whole thing. Perhaps I in fact ate the chip but, because the salsa was so mild, I barely noticed. Yes!

I reopen my legs and peek through. No! The chip is still there, planted on the couch cushion like a flag. I oh-so-casually reach below and yank it out, praying that it hasn't left behind any rogue salsa. Has it?

There is a fortune cookie–shaped red smudge on the couch.

Shoot.

I glance up to see if anyone else has noticed the disaster.

"Isn't it ridiculous?" Joelle is saying, her arms flailing. Karin is laughing, head bobbing along, and Tash is quietly chomping on a peanut.

Why didn't I have a peanut?

None of them are paying attention to me in the slightest. None of the million other people in here seem to have noticed me either. Maybe my braces give me the superpower of being invisible.

"Karin," I whisper, but she doesn't seem to hear.

But Bryan Sanderson—cute, sporty Bryan Sanderson—is looking right at me. Looking right at me and grimacing. Fantastic. I haven't even been introduced to him and I've already managed to disgust him.

"Saw that," he mouths.

I'm pretty sure my cheeks are the color of the salsa, but I mouth back, "What do I do?"

He holds up his right index finger. "Stay there," he tells me, and heads out through the side door into the kitchen.

I bet the couch was expensive. The entire house is sleek, with marble floors and glittering chandeliers. The Kings didn't find this couch at Walmart, I'll tell you that. I bet it was imported from San Francisco or France or Africa or somewhere.

What if the stain doesn't come out? Will I have to pay for the couch? Or, since I have zero money, will my parents have to pay for the couch? Will I be working off the loan for the next twenty years? Will I have to drop out of school and get a job? Am I even qualified to do anything?

Is Bryan coming back? I hope he's coming back. Not just because he looked like he might be planning on helping me, but because he's just so *cute*.

I wait for him, frozen in place, terrified of moving and causing additional havoc. A few moments later, he returns, holding a bottle of water like a trophy. He smiles and says, "Scoot over."

The only plus side to this situation? Since the salsa never made it to my mouth, I am one hundred percent positive there is none stuck in my braces.

I gingerly stand, shuffle to my left, and sit back down, careful not to land on the stain. Bryan plops down to my right. He smells fresh and shampoo-y, like soap that claims it's unscented but really isn't.

"Are you ready?" he asks me out of the side of his mouth, as if he's a ventriloquist.

"What do you have there?"

"Poland Spring orange-flavored sparkling water. And a vinegar-soaked napkin hidden in my sleeve."

Adorable Spiked-Haired Boy is very resourceful. But why is he helping me? He doesn't even know who I am. "Orange-flavored sparkling water?"

He shrugs apologetically. "I couldn't find the club soda."

"But why orange? Are they out of watermelon?"

He laughs.

Yay, I made him laugh! "This is not a laughing matter," I say, and then giggle. My cute-boy giggle is even worse than my regular giggle.

"Are you ready?" he asks.

"You sound like you have a plan."

"I don't plan," he says. "I just do, Devi." His voice is teasing.

He knows my name? "You know my name?" I was not supposed to say that out loud.

"I took a wild guess. I was going to try Katie, but you look like a Devi. A Devi Banks."

I smack him—playfully and, hopefully, flirtatiously—on his arm. His muscled arm. Hello there, muscled arm. Must stop staring at muscled arm. Must also remove my hand from muscled arm.

"Here's what's gonna happen," he says. "I'm going to drench the stain—"

I shush him. "Don't use the S word."

He laughs again. I giggle again.

"I'm going to soak the *discoloration* with the carbonated water."

"That's another S word," I whisper.

"Will you let it slide?"

"Another one!"

"I'll try to be more sly," he says, his eyes crinkling.

"Quit changing the subject and get back to what you want me to do," I order.

"Fine. Step two is to rub the discoloration with the vinegar."

I dubiously look at the stain—er, discoloration. "Are you sure this'll work?"

"No. But I saw it on a TV show."

"If you saw it on TV, it must be true."

He laughs. Again.

I giggle. Again.

He cocks his head to the side and looks at the ceiling. "I think it was club soda and vinegar. Pretty sure."

Good enough for me. I'm pretty sure I'd follow anything he said at this point. "Might as well give it a try."

"But how are we going to do this without anyone noticing? Should I clear the room? Shout 'fire'?"

"Why don't I try to be a bit more subtle? Whoops. Another S word. I'm bad at this."

"I'll forgive you. Again."

"You're the best."

Aw! My body is back to feeling jittery, but this time, it's a good jittery.

He twists off the bottle top and lifts the bottle up to his lips.

"Refreshing?" I ask. He has nice lips. Lips perfect for kissing.

"Definitely," he says. "Celia's serving pretzels outside and they're extra-salty. See? There's a reason I'm drinking watermelon-flavored sparkling water."

"Orange-flavored," I say, correcting him.

If she'd been serving pretzels in here instead of salsa, this whole mess wouldn't have happened. Way to go, Celia. Although then I wouldn't be having cleansing bonding time with Bryan. Way to go, Celia!

"Okay," he says, "your job is to sit facing me, so your knees block the view."

Turn to face him? This is getting better by the second. "Done."

"Now, is anyone watching?"

I scan the many not-paying-attention faces. "All clear."

"Here goes." He whisks the bottle over the spot and wets it. Then he rubs the spot with the napkin. "This should work."

"Promise?" I can't help smiling—but I try to do it without showing any teeth. I really, really hate these things.

"I don't make promises I'm not sure I can keep. But here's hoping."

"Sands!" a muffled voice yells. "We have to go!" Jerome Cohen is waving on the other side of the glass doors that lead to the terrace.

Don't go, don't go!

Bryan lifts his eyebrows, as if to say, You got this handled, or should I stick around?

"Go ahead," I say. "I'll take it from here. Thank you so much for your help." How awesome is he? So awesome. Amazingly awesome. Exceedingly awesome. The awesomest.

He stands up, stretches his arms above him, and gives me one of those fabo smiles. Two dimples and everything. "See you, Devi."

I love that he knows my name. I smile back, remember my braces, and slam my lips closed. Then I smile again. Aw, what the heck?

As I watch him go, my cell phone starts to ring. I check the caller ID and see that it's my number again. Go away! What does she want, to yell at me for coming to the party? Good thing she didn't see the salsa smorgasbord on the couch. Or did she? I should ignore her, like Maya said. I turn off the power. I don't care what the prankster who's calling me has to say; I am *not* going to let her ruin my lovely, romantic, and slightly discolored night.

Bryan was right. The stain disappears. I wish he were still here so I could thank him.

Hmm. I wonder if his technique works on nail polish.

When I'm safe in the backseat of Mr. Caldwell's car, getting a ride home, I turn my phone back on. Eight new messages.

"Hi! It's me! Just wondering what's going on. Call me back."

Here come the neck tingles.

The second one's a hang-up.

Third too.

Fourth: "Actually, I don't know if you can call me back. Can you call me back? I'll call you later."

Fifth: "Why aren't you answering? Where are you? We had a plan. I hope you're not at the party. Maybe you're in the bathroom. Next time you go to the bathroom, take the phone with you. Try to call me back. Otherwise I'll call you back. In like ten minutes."

Sixth: "It's me! I need to speak to you! Urgently!"

"How many messages do you have?" Joelle asks, twisting around to look at me.

"Eight."

"Yikes. Hope it's not your parents."

At this point, I wish it were. I delete the rest of the messages without listening to them.

"Thank you!" I call to Mr. Caldwell when he stops in front of my house. As I hop up the steps, my cell rings. It's my number again.

Enough! This has to end *now*. I press send.

"Where have you been?" she asks.

"Hold on," I say. Since Mr. Caldwell is still waiting, I unlock the front door, wave, go inside, wait until they drive away, and then step back onto the porch. "What?" I bark.

"You went to that party, didn't you?" Weird-Grumpy-and-Possibly-Cruel-Stalker-Prank-Playing Girl says tartly.

I lean against my front door. "Why do you keep calling me?"

"Why would you go to the party even though I told you not to? What is wrong with you?"

"How do you know I went to the party? You were there, weren't you?"

"I told you not to go, but you didn't listen. You have to listen to me, do you understand? I know what's best for you!"

I stand upright, creepies crawling down my spine. I don't know what to do. Call the police? Hello, Officer? A girl told me not to go to Celia's and now she's screaming at me.

She lets out a big sigh. "I guess there's no use getting upset now. What's done is done. It's eleven-thirty there, the same time it is here, which means he's about to call you. When he asks you out, you should say no."

"What are you talking about?" With my free hand, I rub my temples. She's giving me a major migraine. "Can you please stop calling me?"

"No! I have to! I have a plan to save us!"

I shake my head. "What is wrong with you? Who are you?"

"Don't you listen? I'm you! In the future!"

I lose it. "That's impossible! You are not *me* in the future! You are not! You are not!"

"I *am*, and he's going to call you. As soon as you get home from the party, he calls and asks you out. First he's gonna ask if you got the salsa stain off, and then he's gonna ask you to see a movie tomorrow night. And then, after the movie, you guys go bowling. He's obsessed with bowling. Trust me."

She's crazy and needs to be institutionalized immediately. "Nobody is calling me. Nobody but you."

"Bryan is going to call you! Any second!"

"Bryan Sanderson? He's not going to call me. He doesn't even have my number." Wait a sec. "How do you know about the salsa stain? Tash, is this you?" Tash always seems to be taking everything in, even when it doesn't look like she's paying attention.

"I'm not Tash! It's me! You! He got your number from Joelle."

"That's ridiculous."

"Devi. Bryan is going to call you. Trust me, you just got home, you're in your room, and Bryan is about to call. I know."

"I'm not in my room! I'm standing outside my house! On my porch! So there!"

Beep.

"That's him!" she yells. "See for yourself!"

This is ridiculous. Bryan Sanderson is not calling me. "I want you to go away. For good. Good-bye." I click over to the other line. "Hello?"

"Devi? Hey, it's Bryan. The guy from"—he laughs—"the couch."

Omigod. It's Bryan. It's Bryan? My heart races to an inhuman and possibly dangerous speed. "Hi."

"Hey. Is it too late?"

"No, um, it's not too late." Bryan Sanderson is calling me! How did Crazy Stalker Girl know?

"So how'd it go with the salsa?" he asks.

"It worked. Thanks. Thank you." My heart flip-flops. She knew. How did she know?

"Good. Cool. My lift left early from Celia's but I got your number from Joelle. That girl knows everyone, huh?"

I'm too shocked to say anything. I grunt. Very ladylike.

"So, listen, are you around tomorrow night? Do you wanna see that new movie *101 Possibilities?* It's supposed to be good."

A movie. He wants to see a movie. Tomorrow.

"Sure," I say, stunned both that she knew and that he's asking. Bryan! Is! Asking! Me! Out! For tomorrow night!

Beep.

"Great," he says. "Say around eight? Where do you live?"

Beep.

It's her. Of course it's her. "On Sheraton." I want to know how she knew, but I also want to keep talking to cute Bryan!

Beep.

"I know where that is. Near Hedgemonds Park, no?"

The call-waiting stops. She went to voice mail, probably.

"Yup, I'm a two-minute walk from the park."

"They have the best swings," he says.

I giggle. "Are you a connoisseur?"

"I'd like to think so."

Beep.

Omigod, she's just going to keep calling until I answer. And anyway, I want to know how she knew he was going to call me. Maybe he told her? Maybe she likes him and she's jealous? "Bryan, I'm so sorry, but I really have to get this. Can I call you in the morning?"

"Sure. Call me," he says. "Night."

"Night," I say, trying to sound nonchalant, and then click over to my other line. "Do you like Bryan or something? Is that what this is about?" Yes, that must be it. Someone saw me ogling Bryan today at baseball, guessed that I liked him, and now wants to stop us from going out.

"I *don't* like Bryan. I mean, I did like Bryan . . . but I don't anymore. We don't anymore. He ruined our life. But that's not the point." She lets out a sigh. "Did you agree to go out with him?"

As if I'd say no. "It's none of your business," I huff.

She groans. "It most definitely is. You're *me*. I'm *you*. We're the *same* person. Don't you get it?"

"That isn't possible!" If she doesn't like Bryan, why is she calling me? Who *is* she? A mosquito snaps at my arm and I wave it away. "Will you just hold on a sec? I want to go inside. Or you can call me back. Or can I call you back?" If Crazy Stalker Girl gives me her number, maybe I can block her calls.

"I don't think that'll work. I'll just hold."

I unlock the door, kick off my shoes, and tiptoe into the house. I stop when I see the kitchen light on.

"Hello?" I say.

"It's me," my dad says, poking his head out. "Just getting a snack."

He's still dressed in his suit and tie and is holding a plate of lemon chicken. His eyes look tired, like he's spent the last twenty-four hours in front of a computer. His hair is starting to turn gray too. His job is seriously killing him. The bags under his eyes are huge and his suit looks baggy on him. He could use a few plates of lemon chicken.

"Late night?" I ask.

He sighs. "Yeah."

"Mom asleep?"

He nods. "I'm just finishing this and going to bed. I have to go back into the office tomorrow."

"Good night," I say, clutching my phone against my chest. I hope she didn't hear all that. Crazy Girl doesn't need to know any more details about my life.

When I close the door to my room, I pick up the phone and say, "Go on."

"Dad sounds so tired," she says sadly.

She's too much. "Not *Dad*," I say. "My dad. Mine."

"He's my dad too. I'm you. Aren't you paying attention? I can prove it to you."

I swallow. "No thanks."

"I know everything about you. Your bank code is 1016, your mom's birthday."

I gasp. How . . . ? She must have found out my mom's birthday. Mom only keeps the year a secret. I'm sure I'm not the first girl whose bank code is her mother's b-day, right?

"Your computer password is Ivy0805, which is a combination of the name you wish your parents *had* given you instead of naming you after your dad's dead grandmother, and the day you were supposed to be born on, except Mom went into labor two weeks early after having two bowls of Peking Gardens' hot and sour soup."

My whole body is tingling.

"You love Froot Loops right from the box. You also like to eat your pizza upside down so it doesn't burn the top of your mouth. You love extra-sharp cheddar, the white kind, even though you always manage to cut your thumb on the cheese slicer. You're terrified of dogs. You squat when you go to the bathroom at school because you're afraid of getting a disease, and sometimes you pee on the floor by accident."

"That was only once!" Twice. Four times, max.

"Five, actually," she says.

"Okay, five."

"The reason you skipped the holiday party in eighth grade was not because you had a hundred-and-two fever, like you told your cute but dumb ex-boyfriend, Jarred, but because you burnt your upper lip trying to bleach it and gave yourself a red mustache. Maya felt bad for you and stayed home and watched movies with you. You didn't even tell Karin the truth. Speaking of Karin, remember when you went out with Anthony Flare even though you knew she liked him? Oh yeah, you knew. She never told you she did, or admitted to anyone, but you're her best friend. And you did it anyway."

My hands are shaking. No one—I repeat, *no one*—knew that I knew. I don't even think I ever admitted it to myself.

"Do you believe me yet?" she asks.

"I . . ." My head might explode. How can this be? It can't. It just can't.

"Oh, I know an even worse one! When you were six—when *we* were six—we climbed up our dresser and it fell on us, and Dad came running out of the bathroom when he heard the crash, and his pants were down and we saw *everything*!"

"Eewwwwww," I groan, remembering.

She giggles: "He-he-he-he-he."

That giggle cannot be faked.

Holy salsa stain, she's me.

chapter seven

Finally. I got through to her. To me. Hello, confusing. "I can't believe it," Freshman Me says, voice shaking.

"I know!"

"But . . . but . . . how did this happen?"

So I lie back on my twin bed and tell her about how I'd dropped the phone in the fountain.

"It's not that I don't believe you," she says, "but I kind of wish I could see something concrete. You know, as proof."

I look down at the fading brownish spot on my carpet. "The proof is in the nail polish, no? And I tried to test it," I remind her. "I told you not to go to the party."

"Well, I need to know for sure this is real before I start messing with my life. Maybe I should do something and you can tell me what I did. Because you'd see it. In real time. Or you would see it if you were really me in the future."

"Like what?"

She giggles. "If I told you, it wouldn't be a surprise."

I'm not sure how I feel about surprises. "Let's just make sure we're on the same page."

"Like cut my hair," Freshman Me says. "Or pierce my belly button."

"No amateur haircuts," I say quickly. "Remember the bangs disaster? And anyway, hair will grow back in three and a half years. And I'd really rather not get hepatitis."

"What if I carve something into the wall?" she asks.

Now we're talking. "Go for it. But just use a Sharpie. You don't want to slice off a finger. And do it somewhere Mom can't see."

"Like where?"

I scan my room for an appropriate spot. My desk, my mirror, my closet . . . "Behind the dresser?"

"That'll work," she says.

"But don't topple it," I warn. "We don't want Dad running out naked."

We both giggle.

I hear grunting and then "Okay, I've moved the dresser. Now I'm writing something. Can you see? Can you see?"

"Hold on! I'm not there yet." I jump off my bed, run over to the wall, and pull out the dresser. I hope it's there. It has to be there. Is it going to be there? I look up and down the wall. I don't see it. Why don't I see it? Wait! I see it! Written on the wall are the words *Place Desk Here!* My brain goes all fizzy, like I drank too much soda. " 'Place Desk Here'! I see it! I see it!" Hah! She's funny! I'm funny!

"No way!" she screams. "No way!"

I jump up and down. "Way! It's there! I see it! I told you! You're really me!"

"So . . . whatever I do in my life will change *your* life?" she asks. "Which, um, is really *my* life, just not yet?"

"Yes!" The possibilities are endless.

"Wait a sec," Freshman Me says. "Do you remember writing on the wall?"

Huh. I close my eyes and rack my brain. I try to remember holding up the Sharpie or writing on my wall. But I got nada. Nothing. Zilch. I wonder what that means. "Nope," I say. "But obviously I did it. It's right in front of me."

"But do you remember being me? I mean, do you remember being me and talking to yourself as a senior?"

"No. I remember being in freshman year, but I never spoke to me. At least, I don't remember speaking to me." I rub my temples. So that means that my reality changes, but my memories don't. I think. "This is giving me brain freeze."

"I know! Me too!"

"Write something else," I order.

"Okay. What should I say?"

"Surprise me again." I stare at the wall.

"Whoops," she says.

"What happened?"

"I wrote on my thumb," she whimpers. "With the permanent marker."

I lift up my mark-free hand. "Not that permanent."

"Good. 'Kay, hold on."

At first the space next to *Place Desk Here* is blank, but then suddenly it says *This is weird.* "This is weird! I see that!"

"You do? How do you see that? I've only written 'this.' I didn't get to 'is weird' yet."

"Really?" I say. "Now that *is* weird."

"I wonder why," she says, sounding doubtful again. I don't want her going doubtful on me. I don't want her questioning it all over again.

"Maybe my present changes as soon as you go in a new direction in the past. You were sure you were going to write 'This is weird,' so it did it for you."

"But what if I change my mind and write something else instead? Which will you see?"

"Well . . . try, I guess."

"Tell me as soon as you see anything," she says.

As I stare at the wall, the letters change. They don't shake or morph or do anything gradual. They just change, like a flipped channel on the TV. *Is weird* suddenly says *is cool. This is cool.* "I see it! I see it!" So much for permanent marker.

"Already? But I only wrote the 'c'! Wait a sec. Now what do you see?"

Cool changes to *cat*. " 'This is cat'?" I laugh. "What does that even mean?"

"I don't know! But I already wrote the 'c,' so I had to use it."

I shake my head. "But now 'This is cat' is written on our bedroom wall. Forever."

"Er. It is? Until I change it again, you mean."

Whoa, that is too much power for Freshman Me. "From now on, you're not allowed to do anything before discussing it with me."

She giggles. "Yeah, right."

I so wasn't kidding.

"Okay, I believe it now," she says breathlessly. "And I want to know everything. How's Mom? And Dad? And Maya? And Karin?"

I sit down on my carpet and stretch out my legs. "I forgot about Karin."

"How did you forget about Karin? Aren't we still best friends?"

"Not so much." I lie down on my back and look up at the ceiling.

"What happened? Is she okay?"

"She's all right," I say quickly. Then I add, "Actually, I heard she has some major eating issues."

"What? That's terrible! But she's so healthy! She's trying out for the gymnastics team and everything."

"Yeah, well, supposedly the coach is a nutcase and tells all the girls on the team that they have to weigh ninety pounds."

"Couldn't you help her? Tell her the coach was crazy?"

Um, no. "It didn't happen while we were still friends."

"But why aren't you still friends?" she asks, sounding crushed.

"It's a long story." You'll see, I almost add. Sometimes things change. Whether you want them to or not.

"I can't believe it," she says. "That is so sad. What about Joelle and Tash? Am I still friends with them?"

"Not exactly," I admit. I run my fingers up and down the carpet.

"So who are my friends?" she asks, clearly confused. "Do I have a boyfriend? Omigod—is it *Bryan?*"

My stomach twists. "Don't you want to know about what's going on in the world and stuff?"

"Yes! Of course!" she squeals. "Are there talking robots? Have we gone to Mars?"

Hah. How cool would that be? "Uh, no. I'm only three and a half years ahead. Actually, not much has changed. We still have the same president. We still have global warming. Your boobs grew."

"They did?"

"Yeah, 34C. Plus your skin is really good."

"No more pimples?"

"Only when you have your period. The Scarlet T is gone." I giggle again.

"What's the Scarlet T?" she asks.

"Oh, come on! We named it that! It's the line of red pimples on your nose and forehead."

"I do not know what you're talking about. I mean, I know the pimples, unfortunately, just not the name."

"Maybe I haven't named it that yet then."

"I like it," she says. "I think I'll use it."

"What's mine is yours," I say generously.

"What about my braces?" she asks. "They do come off, right?"

"Beginning of sophomore year."

"A whole year of these things? I hate them," she whines.

"I know, but it's worth it," I promise. I peer into my full-length mirror and smile at my perfect teeth. "Trust me. Oh! But do *not* put your retainer in a napkin in the caf next year, 'kay?"

"A napkin? Everyone knows you're not supposed to do that."

Thanks, know-it-all. "Just don't."

"I won't."

"You will," I insist. "Unless you remember not to."

"So I'll remember not to."

"You don't have the best memory," I say. "Maybe you should keep a list. In a notebook. Otherwise you'll end up writing stuff on scrap pieces of paper and you'll find them years later in your jacket pockets. Or, I guess, I'll find them in my jacket pockets." Still, this is going to be amazing. That mental list of things I was making this afternoon? About things I would change if I could talk to my past self? Now I can do it! Too bad I missed the boat on the bang-trimming and the marshmallow fire, though.

"Good point," she says. "I think I have an extra one somewhere around here."

"Check your shelf," I tell her. "That's where you keep them."

"Yeah, I know," she says with a giggle.

I wait for her to tell me she's ready as she rumbles around.

"Got it. Page one. Sophomore year: don't put retainer in a napkin."

"Good. I think I lose it some other time too. But I forget where. Don't worry. It'll come to me. Where are you going to keep the notebook when you're not using it? We don't want anyone else to see it."

"Desk drawer?"

I open my desk drawer and spot a green spiral notebook. I flip it open to the first page and read the only thing currently written on it: *Sophomore year: don't put retainer in a napkin.* "Perfect."

"Super. Now that we've solved the number one problem in my future—the loss of my retainer—can you tell me about other stuff? Like why I'm not friends with Karin, Tash, and Joelle anymore?"

I rub my temples. "You're just not."

"So who are my friends?"

"You don't really have any girlfriends."

"What does that mean? How can I not have *any* friends?"

"You . . . Karin's not the only one with issues."

"Me?" she asks, sounding panicked. "I have issues? What are they? What happens? You have to tell me!"

I'm not sure what I should reveal. It's my job to be the responsible one here. I don't want to break some sort of time-travel law by spilling the sad beans. And I don't want to mess this up. I'm lucky enough to get a second chance. I'm not going to get a third one.

"You have to tell me! Omigod. Am I dead? Do I die?"

I roll my eyes. "You don't die, silly."

"If I'm silly, then so are you. Just promise I'm not dead."

I slap my palm against my forehead. "I'm talking to you, aren't I?"

"Are you an angel? Are you speaking to me from the grave?" She gasps. "Do I get a terminal disease?"

"You do *not* get sick. There is nothing wrong with you. Except being annoying."

"What about Maya? And Mom? And—"

"Everyone's fine." I open my door and look out into the hall. I can see the faint light of TVs coming from my parents' room and from the home office. "Mom's watching the Food Network right now. As usual. The TV is on whenever she's not at Intralearn."

"What's Intralearn?"

"Where Mom works."

"Mom has a job? Really? That's great! How come she finally decided to go back to work?"

"Oh, um . . ." Craptastic. Do I tell her the truth? "It's because Dad . . ."

"Dad what? Oh, God, is Dad okay? Tell me he's okay!"

"You have to calm down," I say. "I can't tell you things if you're going to freak out at all the bad stuff."

"*All the bad stuff*? How much bad stuff is there?"

I probably shouldn't tell her everything. Don't want to overwhelm her. "Dad's fine. Everyone's fine," I say. And it's kind of the truth. Everyone *is* fine. Everyone except me. I blink a few times.

"What's the bad stuff, then?"

I sit back down on my bed. The breakup. The breakup that breaks your heart. That's what I want to save her from.

I want to wrap her up in a fuzzy coat of denial and protect her. "You just fall in love with the wrong guy," I say carefully.

"Who?"

"Bryan."

"Oh. *Oh*."

"Yeah. Write that down, then."

"Write what?"

"Write 'Don't go out with Bryan Sanderson.' " Back to my plan. Take that, Bryan. You have a plan that doesn't involve me; now I have a plan that doesn't involve *you*. And maybe this time Freshman Me will listen to it.

"But what's so bad about Bryan?"

"Everything!" I insist. "Trust me."

"But I like Bryan. He's . . . really nice."

"Devi . . ."

"He is nice!"

"Not that nice," I grumble.

"But how does this all work, anyway? If I don't go out with Bryan, that means that you don't go out with Bryan?"

"Yes. We are the same person."

"Maybe I could go out with him now and break up with him or whatever before the bad stuff happens," she says hopefully.

"No." I square my shoulders. "You have to cancel."

She sighs. "Let's think about that one, okay?"

"No thinking. Just doing. It's too late to phone now anyway. You can call him in the morning."

"Fine—we'll discuss it in the morning."

"No, you'll *do* it in the morning." I clench my hands into fists. "You have to. This is the most important thing you can do. Do you understand?"

"Okay," she says meekly.

Yeah, I've heard that before. "Okay, you promise?"

"I promise." She sighs. "I'll do it."

chapter eight

Saturday, September 10 • • • Freshman Year

My dreams are understandably odd tonight. I wake up at ten-thirty in the morning and check my wall to make sure that I did not, in fact, dream the entire thing.

Nope. *Place Desk Here!* and *This is cat* are still freshly written on my wall—which means I'm supposed to call Bryan to cancel. Sweet, adorable Bryan.

As I step into my bright yellow bathtub—my mom picked the color, saying that it reminded her of lemons and made the room feel fresh—I can't help wondering, Do I really have to cancel? It seems like a crazy thing to do. When you have plans with a guy you have a serious crush on, do you cancel? No, you do not. Although, when your future self tells you it's for the best, you should probably listen. And I promised her. Technically, I also promised Bryan I would go to the movies with him. But I guess promises to my future self beat promises to a guy I've only spoken to twice.

Okay, okay, I'll cancel. Right after I eat something.

I check to see if Dad's briefcase is gone. Yup, he's at work. On a Saturday. I take a handful of Mom's fresh mini lemon muffins—she loves lemons; what can I say?—to the table on the back porch. I am going to cancel. I am. As soon as I finish eating.

When I'm done, I head back to my room. Now what? Now I should cancel. I should. But . . . I really don't want to. I like Bryan.

Instead, I call Maya to see how her party was. She doesn't answer, so I leave a message.

As soon as I hang up, my phone rings. Unfortunately, it's not Maya.

"Helllllllo?" Senior Me drawls. "Did you do it?"

I lie back on my bed. "Can't I just go out with him once? Just once?"

"No!" she cries. "Absolutely not. You have to cancel immediately."

"But he's so nice. And cute. And very knowing in the art of stain removal."

"You'll go out with someone nicer. And cuter."

"Who?"

"I don't know yet, do I?"

"I don't understand what the big deal is," I grumble. "What is *so bad* about Bryan Sanderson?"

She sighs. "It just doesn't work out, okay?"

I slam my fists into the mattress. "But what does that even mean? We don't get married?"

"Of course you don't get married! I'm only seventeen!"

"So then what's the big deal? Just because we break up eventually, we can't hang out tonight? Sounds crazy to me. How long are we together for, anyway?"

"All of high school. You waste your *entire* high school experience on him. Trust me, it's just better to nip this in the bud. Why would you want to even bother going out with him if you know he's going to hurt you? Are you some kind of masochist?"

"Of course not," I say. "But what does he do?"

"He does bad things!" she says, choking up.

"Like what?"

"Stuff!"

"What stuff? I need to know all the details before I change the course of my life."

"He breaks up with us, okay?" she shrieks.

Er. "That's it?"

"No! He's also the reason you're not friends with Karin, Tash, and Joelle anymore."

"Really? He told you not to be friends with them?"

"Kind of. . . . You spend all your time together and blow everyone else off."

"Well, that was dumb of us," I say. "And not really his fault."

"It's not just that." She clears her throat. "He cheats on you. On us."

My heart sinks. "He does?"

"Yes."

"What happens?"

"What difference does it make? It happens. More than once."

"Oh."

"Yeah," she spits out. "I told you. He sucks."

I twist my hair into a bun. I can't believe he would do that to me. Not that I know him that well. I've had two conversations with the guy. But still. I didn't know that sweet salsa guy had it in him to be such a jerk. "I'll do it. I'll call him. What am I telling him exactly?"

"Tell him you could do better than a jerk like him and that you hope he rots in hell."

"I can't say that!"

"He deserves it." She clears her throat again. "Tell him you aren't interested. Now. I'm calling you back in five minutes." She hangs up the phone.

Alrighty then. I'm about to search my calls for his number when my phone rings.

"That wasn't five minutes," I say. "Gimme a sec."

"For what?" Karin asks.

"Hey!"

"Hi! I heard a certain someone asked for your number," she sings. "Tell me everything! Has he called yet? Did he ask you out?"

"He did!" I exclaim. He really did! He likes me! "How did you know?"

"He called Joelle when we were still in the car. I called you two seconds later but I left a voice mail. I thought you would call me as soon as you spoke to him."

"Sorry," I say. "I didn't hear it. And then, after I got off the phone, I was"—too busy drawing on my wall to amuse my future self—"tired."

"So how excited are you?" she squeals.

"So excited," I say. "Except I can't go." Boo.

"What? Why not?"

"Because . . ." Because my future self won't let me go out with him. That probably sounds a bit on the crazy side. "I just . . ." Don't want to go out with a no-good cheater? "I just don't think I'm up for it tonight. I'm not feeling well."

"Oh, no! What's wrong?"

"I'm sick. Really sick. I think it's the flu."

"Well. You don't want to sneeze all over him. Grossness."

"No kidding."

"I guess that means you can't come with me to the mall tomorrow?"

"Oh, um . . ." Boooooooo. "Guess not."

"Yeah, you should probably rest up," she says.

As we hang up, I wonder why I just lied to Karin. Is this how the friend breakup starts? With a lie? Is this why we're no longer friends? Not that I had a choice.

I take a deep breath. Next, Bryan. I don't want to call him. Maybe I should just text him instead. Yes! Then I don't have to talk to him.

Hi Bryan! So sorry! Can't make it tonight.
I'm sick. ☹ Really sorry. I'll see you at
school! ☺ Devi

Done.

I try calling my number to see if this magic cell phone thing works both ways, but it just goes straight to my voice mail. My freshman voice mail.

Guess not.

I leave my cell on my desk and head downstairs to get a glass of juice. Maybe the vitamin C will improve my spirits in addition to my fake cold. I don't know why I feel sad. Bryan hasn't cheated on me yet. I barely even know him.

But now I never will.

chapter nine

Saturday, May 24 • • • Senior Year

"So what's going to happen with prom?" Mom asks me from her seat on the couch.

My back tenses as I open the cupboard. "I'm not going."

She pauses *Best Chef* and turns to look at me. "At all?"

"At all," I say. Instead of looking at her, I take down a glass.

"But what about your dress?" she asks.

A short red prom dress is hanging in my closet. Bryan loved me in red. He thought it made me look sexy. "I don't know. Maybe I'll return it."

"You can't return special-occasion dresses," she says. "Is Bryan still going?"

"He better not be. He wanted us to go as friends but he can forget it. He doesn't get to rip my heart into a trillion pieces and then pop the champagne with me. Let him sit home and be miserable. Like me."

She makes a sad face and then lifts her arms in the air, wanting to give me a hug. "Oh, honey."

"I'll be fine, Mom." Or I would be if Freshman Me would just do what she's supposed to.

"It's still two weeks away. Can you go with someone else? Or maybe with some girlfriends?"

If only I had someone else to go with. If only I had other friends. Although, if I did have other friends, then I'd be with them right now instead of hanging with my mom. "Not a big deal." I turn on the faucet.

And that's when it happens.

The heart bracelet on my arm disappears. One second it's resting comfortably on my wrist, and the next second it's . . . gone.

"My bracelet!" I shriek.

"What bracelet?" my mom asks.

"The one that Bryan got me!" Did it just fall down the drain? I turn the water off and try to spot it.

"Bryan who?" she asks.

"Bryan-Bryan," I·say, sticking my fingers inside.

Mom comes over to me. "Who's Bryan? Have I met him?"

My fingers freeze. Huh? My mom doesn't know who Bryan is?

Wait. The bracelet he got me is gone. My mom seems to have forgotten he exists. Does this mean what I think it means? I look up at my mom. "You really don't know who Bryan is?"

She scrunches her forehead. "Not that I can remember. Is he a friend of yours?"

Oh. My. God. Freshman Me did it. She canceled her plans with Bryan. They're not going out tonight. They never go out. We never go out. There is no bracelet. My mom doesn't know who Bryan is. "You've really never met him?"

"Doesn't ring a bell," she says, frowning.

Holy time warp. "I need to make a call." I hurry up to my room to call Freshman Me. "You did it!" I tell her as soon as she answers. "You rock! My bracelet is gone! And Mom has no memory of Bryan. None. Isn't that crazy? I still remember him, but she has no idea!" I twirl in place, around and around and around. I stop only when I spot the photo. The Halloween picture. Or what was previously the Halloween picture and is now a close-up of Karin, Tash, Joelle, and me—with braces—laughing. We're standing in a driveway. Joelle's arms are outstretched, like she took the shot herself. "The last picture of Bryan is gone too! I think the one here now is of you guys last night at Celia's! It worked. You got rid of him!"

"So that's it?" she asks softly.

I examine the picture to make sure. "Yes. Well done. I'm so proud of you. Of us. We did it! We got rid of Bryan forever!"

"That sounds kind of long."

No Bryan. *No Bryan.* I shiver. Who am I without Bryan? "Oh, no," I say, seeing the wall in front of my bed. My bare wall. Bare arm and bare wall.

"What?" she asks with a twinge of hope in her voice. "He's still there?"

"No, it's not that," I say. "It's my TV. It's gone too."

"What TV? The one in the living room?"

"No, the TV in my room." TV—gone. Bryan—gone.

"When did we get a TV in our room?"

"Forget it." I shake away the weird Bryan-is-gone twinges. "Not important. What's important is that we got rid of Bryan." I glance back at the picture. "A little piece of advice for the notebook? In the future, you should not wear that lipstick with your braces. It looks ridiculous. In fact, you probably shouldn't wear any lipstick. I'd focus on eyeliner if I were you. Which I am."

"I thought it looked good," she squeaks.

"Well, it doesn't. Sorry, Freshman Me."

"Don't call me Freshman Me. It's confusing. Call me Devi."

"*That's* confusing," I tell her. "I'm Devi. Why don't I call you Devorah and I can be Devi?"

"No way," she says. "I don't want to be Devorah. That's what Mom and Dad call us when they're mad."

"Then I'll be Senior and you can be—"

"Junior?"

"I was going to say Frosh."

"Frosh," she repeats. "I like it. I don't like Senior, though."

"Seniorita?"

"No."

"Elder?"

She laughs. "No."

"Genius?" I ask, smiling. "Oh, I know! I'll be Ivy."

"I want to be Ivy too!" she says jealously. "I love the name Ivy!"

"So do I. But we can't both be Ivy. That's the whole point. And I called it first." Technically, I get everything first. And I know everything first. I know everything that is going to happen to her for the next three and a half years.

I know everything that will happen to *everyone* for the next three and a half years.

Or everything that was *supposed* to happen. Until I intervened.

Oh. My. God. If I can stop Bryan and me from dating, I can stop other bad things from happening too. I can fix the entire world. I need to think. To brainstorm. I need a list. "Frosh, I need to call you back," I tell her.

As soon as I hang up, I pull the tattered green notebook out of the drawer, my heart pounding. Frosh's list doesn't have to just be about Bryan and my lost retainer. I can tell Frosh all the bad things that have happened in the world since I was a freshman, and she can stop them from taking place. She can fix them. I'm a modern superhero, rushing over to save the day! I'm Future Girl! All I need is a cape.

I flip to the last page of the notebook and try to think of some of the bad stuff that's gone down in the last three and a half years. I should start with big things. Like wars and famines and hurricanes. And then I'll move on to more specific bad stuff. Like last year when Janice Michael's little brother ate a peanut remnant and had an allergic reaction and fell into a coma. Or last summer when that guy a year ahead of me, Kyle Borster, got drunk, got behind the wheel of his car, and hit a bus, sending three people to the hospital. When Joelle left the water running in the bathtub and flooded her basement. When Karin stopped eating.

Or when my dad got laid off from his job and we lost our health insurance. Maya had to get a job to pay for school because her scholarship wasn't enough, and I got a summer job at Bella, and Mom had to get a job at Intralearn.

It's going to be a long list. But maybe I should leave off the one about Dad. For now, at least. Why should she worry when there's nothing she can do? How could she stop it? Tell Dad not to go to work on firing day?

I spend the rest of the day hunched over the notebook, writing. I can't believe how many sucky things have happened over the last three and a half years. I keep at it until my stomach starts to grumble and I notice that it's gotten dark outside. I stretch my arms in front of me.

Twinkle.

Huh? I grab hold of my arm and stare. The gold bracelet is back on my wrist. What the heck?

I push my chair back and grab the picture frame. The bad lipstick with braces—gone. Which would be good, except that Tash, Karin, and Joelle are also gone. Bryan and I are back in our Halloween costumes, fangs glistening at the camera.

chapter ten

Saturday, September 10 • • • Freshman Year

Through the peephole, I see Bryan in faded jeans and an untucked green shirt, standing at my front door, holding a container of . . . soup.

My heart flips. Omigod. He's here. To see me. With soup. Is that not the sweetest thing ever? What should I do? I know that Senior Me—er, Ivy—would want me to send him away, but . . . how can I possibly turn away a guy who brings me soup? A hot guy who brings me hot soup.

I pull open the door. "Hi!"

"Hey," he says, the tips of his cheeks turning red. "How are you feeling?"

Right. I cough. Twice. "I'm okay. Come in!" He follows me inside and sits down beside me on the couch. "I brought you chicken soup." He holds up the plastic container. "Dorky, I know, but I need you feeling better for next weekend."

"That is so nice," I say. He could not be any cuter. I mean, really. He hands me the container. I'm not sure what to do, so I take it and place it on a magazine on the coffee table.

"So can we do something next weekend? See a movie maybe?"

Yes! I mean, no. "Yes," I say. Definitely yes. I can't turn Bryan down. I just can't. I don't want to.

He gives me a big dimpled smile. "Superb."

My cell begins to ring from my bedroom. I ignore it. "So how's your weekend going?" I ask.

"Uneventful. Played some ball today."

The cell rings again. And again. La, la, la, I can't hear it. When it finally stops, I unclench my shoulders.

Then I hear, "Hello, Devi's phone."

Omigod. My mom just answered my cell. My mother. Just answered. My cell. "Mom, don't!" I scream, but of course it's too late. What does it mean that she answered? Did she recognize my older voice?

"Devi," my mom says, coming down the stairs holding up my phone, a puzzled look in her eye. "It's someone named . . . Ivy? Or Ivan maybe? I couldn't tell if it was a boy or a girl. But she—or he—says it's urgent. Asked if you were talking to a boy, but I told her you weren't. Oh." She comes to a halt behind the couch when she spots Bryan. "I didn't know you had a friend over."

I grab the phone from her hand and hold it behind my back. "Mom, this is my friend Bryan."

Bryan stands up and holds out his hand. "Nice to meet you, Mrs. Banks."

Mom smiles and shakes his hand. "Can I get you something to drink or eat? I just made apple brownies."

"That sounds delicious. Thank you."

Mom disappears into the kitchen and I pick up the phone and press it to my ear. "Can you call back later?" I ask. "I'm kind of busy right now."

"You don't say," she growls. "The bracelet is back on my wrist. The picture is back in its frame. You screwed everything up!"

"But I—I—"

"Tell Bryan to get lost!"

"But I don't want to." I want him to stay. I want to go out with him. I want to see a movie with him!

"Tell him he's a jerk!" she screams in my ear.

I turn around so my back is to him. "He brought me chicken soup," I whisper.

"Spill it over his head!" she yells.

I press the phone more tightly against my ear so that he won't hear. "I don't want to. I want to go out with him," I whisper again.

"Frosh," she says, her voice shaking, "you have to listen to me. Don't waste three and a half years with him. You have so many more important things to do with your time. Don't let him ruin your life."

"But—"

"He breaks your heart," Ivy continues urgently. "You have to trust me."

My eyes feel hot. I don't want to send him away, but

what can I do? How can I not trust my future self? *"Fiiiine,"* I grumble, and then hang up the phone and drop it onto the coffee table. I turn back to Bryan.

"I'm so sorry, Bryan." Now what? I take a deep breath. "I'm not really sick."

His forehead wrinkles. "You're not?"

"No. It's just that . . ." My future self won't let me go out with you? Um, no. "I have a boyfriend." Yes! I have a boyfriend. He can't argue with that, plus it won't hurt his feelings.

He steps back. "I didn't know."

My heart sinks. I know I shouldn't care what he thinks or feels, but I do. I want him to smile again! I miss the dimply smile! "I should have told you. You caught me by surprise when you asked me out and . . . well . . . I'm sorry."

The cell rings again. I ignore it.

He cocks his head to the side. "Does that mean you don't want the soup? It's not homemade or anything, but it's still good."

"I'm glad it's not homemade," I tell him. "Then I'd feel *really* bad."

He laughs. "Store-bought, I swear."

"Phewf." I smile. "I *am* really sorry."

"I get it. No problem." Bryan starts walking to the foyer.

Mom peeks out from the kitchen. "Leaving already? Don't you want an apple brownie?"

"You should have an apple brownie," I say. It's the least I can offer.

"In exchange for the soup?" he asks.

"Sure. It's homemade," I tell him. "My mom's secret recipe."

"I'd love one, thank you. But I'm actually on my way out. I was just stopping by." He turns to me, biting the bottom of his lower lip. "So, I'll see you at school?"

"Yup. Monday it is."

"Where are you off to?" my mom asks.

Yeah, Bryan, where are you off to?

"Just bowling," he says.

My stomach free-falls. Who's he going bowling with? Is he cheating on me already?

"I'll pack you one for the road," my mom says, disappearing back into the kitchen.

"I may have to share it with the guys, though," he adds.

Oh, good. Guys. Not that it matters.

Mom returns with a brown paper lunch bag stuffed with goodies, hands it to him, and winks. "Enjoy."

"Thank you. I'm sure I will. Enjoy the soup," he tells me.

"Good night," I say, swallowing the brownie-sized lump in my throat. As I close the door behind him, my phone immediately starts ringing again. "He's gone, okay?" I snap.

"I know! The picture and gold bracelet are gone too. Did you spill the soup on him?"

"No, I did not. Mom gave him brownies." I put the container of soup into the fridge.

"Not her apple brownies! I loved her apple brownies. She never makes them anymore. I can't believe she wasted her brownies on him. Have another one for me?"

I take another brownie.

"Do you want to watch a movie?" Mom asks me.

"Yeah," I tell her. Then I yawn. Loudly. This whole day has exhausted me. "Ivy, do you mind if we hang up now that the Bryan issue is taken care of? I'm tired and I can't really watch and talk at the same time."

"Yeah, yeah, go relax. You deserve it. Oh, and, Frosh, in the future—" She laughs. "In your future, I mean, don't leave your phone lying around. I had to mask my voice when Mom answered or she would have known something was up for sure."

"Right. Sorry about that."

"And don't tell Mom about me. Don't tell anyone."

"Why shouldn't I?" I say.

"I think it's better to keep it HC for now, no? Look how freaked out you got. The wish was that I could speak to you. Not to everyone in the past. I don't want to risk messing things up."

"Wait—what's HC?"

"Seriously?"

"Is that a new expression?"

"It means 'highly classified.' "

"Oh. Cool." Scarlet T, HC . . . I can start a dictionary of the future.

"Just don't tell anyone," she says. "I won't either. It'll be our secret."

"Okay." I switch the phone to my other ear. "So what happens now?"

"What do you mean?"

"Am I going to . . . speak to you again?"

She laughs. "Yeah! Of course. Tomorrow. We need to make sure Bryan stays gone. He's like a cockroach."

My heart beats a little faster. So my life will now be run by the Bryan police? Just kidding. Of course I want to talk to her again. She's me in the future. I'm the luckiest girl in the world.

"I'll call you at lunch," she says. "I have a whole list of stuff I need you to add to your list. You're going to save the world. So get a good night's sleep tonight. You're going to need your rest."

"Fabo," I say.

"Have one last brownie, 'kay?"

"You're going to make me gain twenty pounds."

"Trust me, I'll let you know if I gain twenty pounds."

I laugh before hanging up.

I'm glad she's happy. Really, I am. And she must know what's best for me. She has to. Right?

Then why do I feel so . . . cold? I pull a knit blanket over my legs and hug my knees into my chest. It doesn't help.

I throw off the blanket. I know what will warm me up. A bowl of soup.

chapter eleven

Monday, May 26 • • • Senior Year

It's going to be a great Monday.

I step outside my house and take a deep breath. The sun is shining. The birds are chirping. The ex-boyfriend who ruined my life is no longer my ex-boyfriend. I'm going to be the girl I've always wanted to be—with the name I've always wanted. The possibilities are endless.

Sure, I have to walk to school instead of getting a lift from Bryan. And I'll have to sit by myself in the cafeteria. And I have a slight unexplained rash on my chin. But I can take it.

The Halloween picture of Bryan and the heart bracelet did not return yesterday. It was a Bryan-free day. I spent most of it giving Frosh a list of things she needs to fix to make Florence—and the world—a better place. Just seventy-three things. I'm starting small.

"But how am I supposed to stop Kyle Borster from getting drunk and then driving?" she asked.

"Hide his keys! Or tell him that he's going to regret it later when his three friends are in the ICU after he hits a bus."

"But why will he listen to me?" she asked, sounding overwhelmed.

"We'll figure something out," I told her. "We have two years to come up with a plan." We have lots of time for most of the items, actually. We'll figure everything out together.

After lots of trial and error, we came up with a way Frosh could get in contact with me, since she didn't seem to be able to call. "Text yourself," I told her. "Type a text to yourself, send it, then save it."

" 'Kay, hold on. I'm sending it!" A few seconds later, she shrieked, "I got it!"

"Save it!" I cried.

Hmm. The only text on my phone was the one from me. Time travel weirdness? Or was I my only friend?

You are awesome. Why, yes I am. I also figured out that I can reply to her texts and send her new ones.

Honk! Honk! Honk!

I stop in my tracks. Bryan?

It's a silver Honda Civic. Joelle and Karin are in the front. Why are they here? Are they picking up a neighbor?

Honk! Honk! Honk!

I glance around the street to see if there's someone else they may be waving at. Besides a geriatric mowing his lawn,

I'm the only one here. They seem to be waving and honking at me.

Joelle rolls down her window. "Hey! We gotta move. We still have to pick up Tash, and we need our Kogurt Juices!"

Why are they picking me up when I've barely spoken to them in three and a half years? And I drink Kogurt Juice?

"Come on, slowpoke," Karin says.

Oh. My. God. Does this mean what I think it does? I hurry over to the car, open the door to the backseat, and slide in. "Hi," I say, trying to keep my voice steady. If I never went out with Bryan, then I never stopped being friends with Karin, Tash, and Joelle. I do have friends! Hah!

Best. News. Ever. I want to wrap my arms around both of them and pull them into a bear hug. But I control myself.

Karin turns toward me and smiles. "Hi!"

I try not to visibly cringe. Even though I see Karin every day at school, I haven't been this close to her since she got so skinny. Her arms are like twigs. Her face is hollow-looking. When we were younger, I never thought her nose was too wide, but on her new face, it looks twice the size. I'm glad it's on my list.

"What is up with your phone?" she asks. "I called you a million times yesterday. There's not even a voice mail."

"Oh. It's . . . compromised." I hope my mom won't try to get in touch. She might force me to get a new one.

"Are you still reeling from this weekend?" she asks.

Maybe they heard about the breakup and are trying to

be nice. "Guess the jerk told everyone he broke up with me," I mumble.

Joelle looks at me in her rearview mirror. "Jerk?" she asks. "What jerk?"

"The jerk! Bryan." Wait. Stop. What am I saying? The entire relationship—including the grand finale—is now a figment of my imagination. Must remember that.

They're staring at me blankly. "What's she talking about?" Joelle asks.

"I have no idea," Karin says. "Are you talking about Bryan Sanderson?"

"Er, never mind," I say quickly.

"Did you hit your head or something?" Joelle asks, laughing. "When did you go out with Karin's ex?"

"Karin's what?" I blurt out. Karin went out with Bryan Sanderson? My Bryan? Excuse me?

"I'd barely call him an ex," Karin says, laughing. "We were together for like two months."

I try to keep the stricken look off my face. Deep breath. Deep breath. So they were briefly together. It doesn't matter. It's over. For both of us.

"Maybe you had more fun on Friday night than I even thought," Joelle says. "I know you hooked up with Harry, but I didn't know about Bryan—"

"I did not hook up with Bryan!" My jaw drops. Harry who? Harry . . . Travis? "Wait. I hooked up with Harry Travis?"

They both laugh. "Were you drunk?" Karin asks. "I

wouldn't have let you hook up with a guy if I thought you were drunk."

I hooked up with Harry Travis on Friday? I do not remember that. Wasn't I home on Friday waiting to talk to Frosh? At least I thought I was. Unless now everything's changed . . .

But still. I can't believe I would kiss another guy when I just broke up with Bryan! Although Harry Travis is seriously hot. Or at least, he was the last time I saw him—when I hid from him on Friday at the mall. And anyway, I didn't just break up with Bryan. Technically, the girl who broke up with Bryan is not the same girl who hooked up with Harry. For all I know, the girl who hooked up with Harry has been in love with Harry for the last three and a half years.

How am I ever going to know what Frosh has been up to since freshman year if all I have are my original memories?

"I wasn't drunk," I say eventually. "I'm just joking with you! Ha-ha, totally kidding. I completely remember hooking up with Harry." Yeah. Sure I do. "But I never hooked up with Bryan. Ever. Never ever."

"You can if you want to," Karin tells me. "Honestly, I wouldn't care. You know we only hooked up a few times."

I swallow the lump of vomit in my throat.

"Have you spoken to him since?" Joelle asks me.

"Bryan?" I ask.

"No. Harry."

Er. "I don't think so." Did I? I'd check my caller ID if my phone worked properly. But if it worked properly, I certainly would not be getting a call from Harry Travis. "I always wondered what it would be like kissing Harry."

Joelle clucks her tongue. "It wasn't like it was your first time."

This keeps getting better and better. "It wasn't?"

"Hello?" Karin cries. "Don't you remember Halloween?"

I *remember* taking Bryan's little cousins trick-or-treating. I *remember* them puking in the backseat of Bryan's new bright blue Jetta—yet another sorry-I-live-in-another-country gift from his dad. "Of course I do. Tell me the story, though—I want to hear your version."

Karin laughs. "My version of how you and Harry made out in Celia King's parents' bedroom at her Halloween party?"

That girl has a lot of parties. Aren't her parents ever home? I hope I stayed off her couch this time. "Right," I say. I guess everyone else has new memories. Memories of the updated and improved me.

I lay my head back on the seat. I've kissed Harry Travis. Twice. Twice that I know about. Wait! I run my hand along my chin. The redness is from Harry's stubble!

"I need you guys to come over this week," Joelle says, pulling into Tash's driveway. "I'm done making my prom dress and I want to know what you think. Now all I need is Jerome to ask me, and I'll be all set. Did I tell you how incredible his show was last night? I swear, he's going to be famous."

I'm hooking up with other guys. I never went out with Bryan. I'm being invited to Joelle's. I'm still best friends with Karin.

We pull up at Tash's front door.

And Tash.

Tash waves from the door, not looking the least bit surprised to see me. "Hi, ladies," she says, opening the car door. She's wearing the same uniform I've seen her in for the last four years: jeans and a black shirt. She squeezes in beside me and pats my knee. "So, you and Hot Harry just can't keep your hands off each other, huh?"

Karin laughs. "She doesn't remember."

"She needs an extra shot of wheatgrass in her banana smoothie," Joelle says, hitting the gas.

"To Kogurt Juice," I cheer, trying to keep out any images of Bryan and Karin. Must focus on the good. New drink. New romance. New—make that old—friends.

chapter twelve

Monday, September 12 • • • Freshman Year

Bryan chooses today to have lunch in school. I secretly watch him and Jerome Cohen head outside and sit on a new wooden bench. The school just renovated the outside area over the summer.

"So are you going out with him next weekend?" Joelle asks, sliding into her seat. "He's adorable."

"No. He's not the right guy for me," I say with more certainty than I feel.

"To each her own," she says, and bites into a chicken finger. "Does that mean you guys won't be doubling with me and Jerome? If Jerome ever notices me?"

"I'm sure Jerome will notice you. I don't think anyone could not notice your insanely awesome outfit." Today she's wearing thigh-high boots and a navy slip dress.

"I'm starving," Karin says, chomping into her tuna sandwich. "I got up early to practice my backflip."

"Where are the tryouts?" Tash asks.

"Gym," she says between bites.

I watch her swallow. I watch her relish her sandwich. I think about number nine on Ivy's list.

If she wasn't on the gymnastics team, then Karin wouldn't have an eating disorder. This is the perfect opportunity to save her!

"Are you sure you want to be on the team?" I blurt out.

All three of them stare at me.

Karin takes a big sip of juice. "Yeah. Why wouldn't I be?"

Because it's going to make you sick. "I heard about a girl who joined the team and became totally anorexic 'cause the coach pressured her so much."

Karin's eyes widen. "Really? Who?"

Ack. "A friend of . . . Maya's. That's what Maya said. Yup. I spoke to her last night and she asked about you and she did not think being on the gymnastics team was a good idea. No, she did not."

Karin's shoulders slump. "I had no idea. Can we call her? I'd love to ask her for more details."

"We could, but she's so busy today. All week, actually. She has a crazy amount of work. She said she was going to be in the library and that her phone would be turned off." I shrug. If she calls now, I'm going to be in serious trouble. But I just spoke to her last night, so she probably won't.

Karin turns to Joelle. "What should I do?"

"I have heard that the coach is a grouch," Joelle admits. "And that the girls on the team all have eating disorders. I didn't want to say anything because you were so set on trying out, but that's the word on the street."

Karin sighs. "I can't imagine not doing a sport this year. I already missed soccer last week. I guess there's tennis in the spring. . . ."

"You probably shouldn't be too hasty," Tash says. "Why don't you go to tryouts and see for yourself? Trying out doesn't mean you have to be on the team."

Karin rests her chin in the palm of her hand. "I might not even make it."

No, no, no. "You'll make it," I say. That's the problem. "Wait! What about . . . cheer?"

Joelle almost spits out her juice. "You want Karin to be a cheerleader?"

"It's a sport," I say, warming to the idea. The cheerleaders I've seen around school so far seem to have surprisingly normal body weights. "And she loves cheerleading. How many times have we watched *Bring It On?* And *Bring It On Again?* And *Bring It On Until We Drop with Exhaustion?* She'd be amazing at it. She's flexible and she can dance and it would be fun. Why not?"

Joelle crosses her arms. "She's too smart to be a cheerleader."

"I'm not pretty enough to be a cheerleader," Karin adds.

I shake my head. "You are too pretty enough. You're hot. And saying all cheerleaders are dumb is like saying all geniuses are nerdy. Look at Tash here!"

"I am kind of nerdy," Tash says with a half smile.

"You are not! Anyway, cheering is a fabo way to meet guys. Come on. There's no risk in trying out."

"Only complete social mortification," Karin says.

"You'd be a great cheerleader," I promise. "We'll come cheer you on at tryouts!"

"You *would* be a great cheerleader," Tash adds.

Karin turns to Joelle. "What do you think?"

Joelle narrows her eyes. "If you ditch us for your cheery friends, I'm going to be pissed."

Karin's eyes widen. "I would never ditch my friends!"

"Then go for it," Joelle says.

"Go for it," I echo.

Karen smiles. "Okay. I think I will."

Ivy is going to be so proud of me. I just saved Karin. I know it.

chapter thirteen

Monday, May 26 • • • Senior Year

"I'll see you at our table at lunch!" Karin calls out to me in the hallway before fourth period. Yes! Guess I won't be sitting alone after all.

After finding a seat in French, I zone out, thinking about my new life. Before today, my lunches were normally spent at Subway, where Bryan and I sat at the table by the far window. Bryan ordered extra mayo. I ordered extra mustard and usually got it on my shirt. And his shirt. Or we took his car through the drive-through at McDonald's and got two Happy Meals, extra ketchup for the fries. Or sometimes, if my mom happened to make something good the night before, which was rare these days, I'd pack up two portions and we'd eat them outside on the wooden bench. Our bench. He even carved our initials into it freshman year. *BTS + DAB*. He always included our middle initials, since without his, his initials are BS. Hah. It was always just the two of us.

Bryan had strep throat for a week sophomore year. I sat with Karin, Joelle, and Tash on Monday and Tuesday, but by Wednesday, it was awkward city and I ate by myself in the library.

I was so pathetic.

We both were. He stayed friends with Jerome, and still played ball, but mostly it was about me.

Last summer his mom made him go on a ten-day cruise through South America for his grandparents' fifty-year anniversary, and all the cousins and aunts and family members were invited. Wives and husbands and fiancés. Everyone official. Everyone except me. He spent the whole trip in the computer room IM'ing me. Afterward, Bryan's mom said that she was never doing that again. That he was a walking misery the entire time. She said next time they went on a family vacation, they were either bringing me along or leaving him at home.

I briefly close my eyes. Guess he's over that now. I bet in this new reality, he had an amazing time on the cruise. Devi who?

I twirl my pencil between my fingers as class drones on and on. It's a good thing classes don't count at this point. Stupid State—aka Stulen State—has already accepted me. Not that that's an achievement. The acceptance rate is 100 percent—they'll take anyone.

Hmmm. Maybe I don't have to go to Stulen. Frosh helped me get rid of Bryan and reconnect with my friends. Maybe she can help me get into a better college too. . . .

When the bell rings, I pack away my books. In the hall,

I pass the committee selling tickets to "Wild West Senior Prom—next Friday!" I look away as fast as I can. But then I look back. I know I'm not going to prom with Bryan . . . but am I going at all? Maybe I'm going to prom with someone else. Harry, maybe? Or maybe we're going all girls! Four best friends in a limo. No dates. Who needs dates, anyway? How to find out without appearing like I've blacked out for the last six months? I need to check my social networks and e-mails. There must be some info in there about this. Prom is in less than two weeks! I dump my books into my locker.

As soon as I step into the caf, I look for my friends. My new/old BFFs. Instead, I run smack into Harry Travis. Oh, God.

He looks just like I remembered, before I learned that we made out. Dark-haired. Still hot. Stubbled. He gives me an intense gaze and then puts his hand on the small of my back, in a much-too-familiar way. "Hey, babe," he says.

Harry Travis is touching my back! In school. In the caf. "H-hi. Harry."

Is he going to try to kiss me right here? Oh. My. God. He can't. My face is still raw. Anyway, Bryan could see. Not that Bryan would care. This Bryan. Old Bryan would have punched his lights out.

But still! This is weird! Really weird! Why is he groping me in the middle of the cafeteria? He's invading my personal space. Oh, God, I don't even know what we did. Did we just kiss? Did we do more? His hand is currently rubbing my back—a back he seems awfully familiar with. What else is he familiar with? I think I'm going to be sick.

"Want to take a drive?"

"Um . . . I can't. Sorry! I actually have to go," I mumble, squirming away from his grasp and hurrying diagonally through the cafeteria and out the door into the yard, where I spot the wooden bench. My bench. Our bench.

I drop to the seat of the bench and it still feels safe. Safer than the cafeteria. My fingers roam the wood to see if Bryan's carving is still there, but the bench is smooth. I swallow the lump in my throat. Will it ever completely go away? What's the point of getting rid of my entire relationship with Bryan if my chest still feels like a block of cement is pressed against it?

What now? I should call Frosh. I told her I'd call her at lunch. I dial my number, but it goes straight to voice mail. What is wrong with her? Why isn't she answering? Oh, crap. She has freshman/sophomore lunch, which is over. This is junior/senior lunch. I can't do anything right.

I pull out my phone and type in `Hi! Sorry I missed u. Will call u after school! XO me.`

It might be weird to send myself hugs and kisses, but I deserve some love. Some non-Harry-Travis-personal-space-invading love.

"Hey, Dev," I hear. My heart stops. Bryan?

I look up. It's Jerome Cohen. Just Jerome Cohen.

He's wearing a green T-shirt for his band, the Spanks. He plays the drums. When Bryan and I first hooked up— when Jerome was with Joelle—Bryan was thinking about taking up the drums too, but that never happened. He was too busy with me. "Can we hang here?" he asks.

"Who's 'we'?" I ask quickly.

"Just me and Sands." He swings his lunch bag in circles, to whatever rhythm is in his head.

I jump off the bench like it's on fire. "All yours. I need to . . . do stuff. Bye." I hurry back inside like I'm trying out for the track team. I spot Joelle and Tash at the table beside the window. A primo table. Not bad, girls. I sit down beside them. I'll get something to eat in a minute.

"What just happened?" Joelle asks me.

"With what?"

"With Jerome! I saw you talking to him outside. Did he say anything about me?"

I shake my head. "Sorry."

She shrugs. "You really should have come with me to the show last night. He rocked the guitar."

Huh? "Isn't he the drummer?"

She gives me a weird look. "Noooo. Bryan Sanderson's the drummer."

"Since when?" I shriek.

"Since . . . always? I don't know. You've been to their shows. Don't you remember? That's where he and Karin first hooked up."

Way too much information. "Where is Karin?" I ask, trying to keep this morning's Kogurt Juice down. "She said she'd meet us here, right?"

"She has cheer at lunch on Mondays."

"She's a cheerleader?" I ask. "Since when?"

They both look at me strangely. "We've only gone to all of her games," Joelle says.

"We have? I mean . . . we have! Of course! I'm just kidding. Ha-ha." My mind is racing. Karin did not used to be a cheerleader. This I would have noticed. This change has got to be Frosh-related.

My stomach growls, and I order and eat a slice of pizza—upside down, of course—all the while wondering what Frosh said to put this in motion. We're about to pack up and head back to our lockers when I spot Karin bounding toward us, her ringlets flying.

"Hi!" she chirps. "Wanted to check in with you ladies before the bell rang." She flounces down beside me.

I stare. She looks . . . different from this morning. What's going on?

She smiles and grabs one of my fries.

She's eating fries?

What is it about her that's off? Has she changed her hair or something? I give her the once-over. Her arms and legs aren't as brittle-looking. They have more meat on them. Like they used to when we were freshmen. And they're tanned. Very tanned. It's sunny outside, but not *that* sunny. "How come you're so . . . tanned?" I ask.

"I'm so not," she says, shaking her head. "I was just thinking that I need to pay the tanning salon a visit. Anyone wanna come with me after school?"

"No. I'll pass," Joelle says. Tash and I shake our heads.

But there's something more. Karin's face looks different. Rounder. Her cheeks are fuller. She definitely looks healthier. But that's not it.

"Karin!" I scream. "Your nose!" Her nose is perfectly

straight. Perfectly. Straight. And narrow. What happened to the curve? What happened to the wideness?

Her fingers flutter to her face. "Did something happen during cheer? Tell me no!"

"Nothing happened," Joelle says. "It looks fine."

"It just looks so straight," I blurt out. "And narrow."

She removes her hand and laughs. "Good. It wasn't cheap."

Oh. My. God. I steady my hands on the table. "Karin, remind me, when did you get it done?"

"My sixteenth birthday. Remember? You brought a cake to the hospital."

"Right," I say. How thoughtful of me.

"Dr. Honig is the best," she says. "We booked him for my graduation present too."

"Your what?" I have a bad feeling about this.

"You know," she says, and then lowers her voice. "My boobs."

Oh, God. Oh, no.

"I have to get something from my locker," I gasp to the girls, and then hurry out of the caf. Back at my locker, I slide to the ground, pull out my phone, and hit send.

It goes straight to voice mail. I hang up and type out a text instead.

`Frosh!` I write. `What the @#%* did you do?`

chapter fourteen

Monday, September 12 • • • Freshman Year

I'm sitting on the bleachers in the gym with Joelle and
Tash, watching Karin try out, when my phone rings. It's my
number.

"Hi!" I say. "I just turned my phone on. Did you forget
about me at lunch?"

"I guess you didn't—"

The rest of her sentence is drowned out by the tryees'
screaming at the top of their lungs, "*Went down to the river!
And I started to drown! And I thought about the Florence Fins!
And I couldn't go down!*"

Karin is kicking river butt. She's definitely going to
make the team. I'm a genius. "Repeat what you said!" I yell.
"It's loud in here!"

"I—"

"*Said one, two, three, four, five, the Florence Fins don't take no jive, said six, seven, eight, nine, ten, let's start this cheer all over again!"*

I block the ear that doesn't have the cell pressed against it. "Sorry, I missed it again. Repeat?"

"Where are you?"

"Cheerleading tryouts!"

"What? Why?"

"Actually—"

"Went down to the river! And I started to drown! And I thought about the Blue Hill Lions and I went straight down! Said one—"

"This is ridiculous!" she yells. "Go somewhere quiet!"

"Hold on, bossy-pants." I turn to Tash and Joelle. "I'll be right back." I maneuver my way off the bleachers and into the hall. "What's up? Where are you?"

"I'm walking home and getting some air," she snaps. "Not screwing up the future like you."

Uh-oh. "What are you talking about?"

"Did you see my texts?"

"No. Hold on a sec." I pull the phone away from me and flip through. Two texts. The last one is not as loving as the first.

"Tell me what you did to Karin. And how cheerleading is involved."

"I saved her!" I say. "Why? What happened? Did she hurt herself in cheer or something? She didn't break a leg, did she?"

"Why are you even at cheer tryouts?" she asks. "I don't understand what happened. Can you start at the beginning?"

I switch the cell to my other ear, take a deep breath, and report all that's gone on from lunch until now.

"Well, she makes it," Ivy says when I'm done. "She's still a cheerleader."

It worked! It worked! Wahoo! "That's great! Does she still have an eating disorder?"

"Nope."

Yay! I cured her! "What's the problem, then? I did what I was supposed to do, didn't I? Wait. Does she ditch us? Does she become all obsessed with her cheerleader friends and forget about us?"

"Also nope."

"So why do you sound so annoyed?"

She sighs. "She got a nose job."

I almost drop the phone. "Oh."

"Oh, yeah."

"But why?"

"I don't know. I'm assuming it has something to do with cheerleading, though."

"But she doesn't have a big nose," I say, still in disbelief.

"She always thought she did."

"But she doesn't!"

"Too late now!"

"I don't know what to say." I chew on my bottom lip. "But maybe it's not too late. Maybe I can fix it. And anyway, a nose job is better than an eating disorder, isn't it?"

"I guess so," Ivy says. "Relatively healthier. Her body definitely looks healthier. Her skin doesn't. It looks like leather."

I pause. "I have no idea what that means."

"She's tanned. Fake tanned. It looks like she lives in a tanning booth."

"That's still better than being anorexic," I say. "I still helped her. Didn't I?"

"I'm not so sure. Guess what her parents are getting her for graduation."

"A car?" How cool would that be? Maybe I'll get a car too!

"A boob job."

"What?"

"A boob job."

I did not see that one coming. "Whoops."

"Yeah. Whoops. Big whoops."

"I swear I didn't know that was going to happen," I say.

"I'm sure you didn't. And I understand why you stopped her from trying out for gymnastics. But from now on you should run any changes to the past by me first. And I think we just learned a bit of a time-travel lesson, don't you? Trying to fix things can really mess them up."

"Shoot," I say. "So what now?"

"You need to stop her from trying out for cheer."

I can still hear the screaming from inside. "I think it's too late. And anyway, cosmetic surgery is still better than anorexia."

"Yeah, but they're both kind of craptastic. You really will have to discuss these things with me."

"But what about the rest of the list? The seventy-two things we're still supposed to fix?"

"I'd hardly call Karin fixed. And I don't know about the rest anymore. . . . What if you make things worse? Let's hold off on the list for the time being. And from now on, you have to run everything by me. Everything."

Yes, she's mentioned that already. Three times. I shuffle my feet. Just because she's older, does that make her the boss? "But—"

"No buts. Karin is getting a boob job and it's your fault," she snaps.

"She hasn't had the surgery yet. Maybe you can convince her not to."

"I'll have to fix your screwup somehow, won't I?"

I roll my eyes. What does she know? She didn't even have friends two days ago. There's more cheering behind the door. "I think I should get back inside. Unlike you, I want to support my friends."

"Oh, God." I hear a sharp intake of breath. "I have to go. It's Bryan."

"But you guys broke—I mean—"

She hangs up.

Now what do I do? I can't let my best friend become a plastic-surgery junkie. I need to fix this. I need a plan.

chapter fifteen

Monday, May 26 • • • Senior Year

I'm on Fleet, halfway between school and home, and Bryan is half a block up, beside a stop sign. He's wearing his green shirt—my favorite color on him—and he's smiling. I can see his dimples from here. Bryan, my Bryan.

Exept he's holding hands with Celia King. I stop in my tracks. What. Is. He. Doing? Why is he touching her? We hate Celia! She's annoying! The only thing we like about her is that we met at her house! Otherwise we think she's a snobby party girl who wears too much glitter and turns every compliment she gives into an insult.

He leans over. And kisses her.

Oh. My. God.

My legs freeze. My arms freeze. My blood is liquid ice. Hasn't he already done enough damage? Is he trying to give me a heart attack? He lifts his hand and runs it through the back of her hair, like he does with me.

Like he did with me. Or like he didn't do with me any-more. I take two steps back, as if he just drop-kicked me in the stomach. I need to sit down. I need to get home. If I click my heels together, can I go home? Please? Stranger things have happened this week.

I try. It doesn't work.

I need to run. Home. Now. I turn at the next corner, a slightly longer route home, and run. My eyes are pricking with tears, but I'm not going to cry. The image of them kiss-ing is still burning my eyes. But I won't cry. If I can just get home, then I won't cry.

My heart pounds angrily against my rib cage, but I don't stop until I'm in my house, in my room, on my bed.

I never thought I'd feel this sick. Seeing him with an-other girl—imagining him with another girl—feels even worse than his breaking up with me. Feels worse than any-thing.

I have a secret. I lied to Frosh.

Bryan never cheated on me.

What else was I supposed to say? She wasn't listening to me! She would have gone out with him. I had to tell her something that she could grasp. Something bad. It was bet-ter than making up something worse, like that he was a drug addict or a bank robber or something.

I wouldn't have said that. Though it did cross my mind.

But how else could I explain? You can't understand what it feels like to have your heart stomped on until you've been through it yourself.

She wouldn't have understood the truth: that he broke

up with me not because he doesn't love me—so he said—but because he wants to see who he is without me. Because even though we had decided to go to Stulen together, he decided to try something new, something else, something different. Because he thought it was time for a change. Because his dad convinced him to go to college in Montreal, where his dad lives and where SAT scores don't matter. Because he made plans that didn't include me. Because he's leaving me. Without anything.

"Who knows?" he said to me the night of our breakup. "If we're meant to be, maybe we'll get back together one day. But right now, this is what I have to do. It's not about you. It's about me."

That was the problem, though, wasn't it? Everything I did was about him.

I flip over onto my back and bang my fists into my duvet.

Someone who loves you doesn't leave you. I'm better off without him.

And now he has a new girlfriend. Or an old girlfriend. Of course he has a girlfriend. Why shouldn't he? Just because I don't have photos of him in my bedroom doesn't mean someone else doesn't. I wonder how long they've been together. Are they in love? Did he have feelings for her when he was with me?

Maybe I was right after all. Maybe he *did* cheat on me. Jerk.

I wonder what happened to all the other frames I tossed. Is he gone from those photos too? I rummage through the garbage and pull them out.

They're all of Karin, Tash, Joelle, and me. Us holding up chopsticks and eating sushi. Us outside a school dance. Us in sleeping bags, making kissy faces at the camera.

Fun. But Bryan?

He's gone. Still gone. And the lump in my throat? Still there.

I look down at my bare wrist. I look up at my bulletin board. There are pictures of me and the girls, birthday cards I don't remember getting, collages of words and pictures I don't understand or remember the importance of. A picture of Harry Travis's head on a cartoon body.

The card Bryan made me for our second anniversary. Gone. The card he got me for Valentine's Day. Gone. The acceptance letter from Stupid State that was tacked to my bulletin board. Gone.

Wait a sec. I jump into a sitting position. Instead of the white sheet of paper congratulating me for getting into Stupid, tacked to my bulletin board is a mint green paper.

It says *Congratulations! You've been accepted to Ballor State!*

I have?

I jump up and pull it from the board. Yup. It definitely says that I've been accepted to Ballor. Sure, Ballor is a fourth-tier school, but it's better than Stulen. It doesn't accept everyone.

How did *that* happen?

Maybe . . . because I didn't spend all my time hanging out with Bryan, I spent more time studying. And by spending more time studying, I got better grades and got into Ballor.

Maya was right all along.

If I apply myself this time around, I don't have to have a B-minus average. I could have an A average. Or an A-plus average. Maya doesn't have to be the only Banks girl to get into a good college. I can get into one too.

By not dating Bryan, I can change more than my relationship history. And my friendship history. I can change my college acceptance.

With Frosh on my side, I can go anywhere I want. UCLA, maybe. Why not? If Maya can go, why can't I? I don't have to be just the pretty Banks girl. I could be the smart one too.

There are a million possibilities.

I won't even have to retake my SATs or anything. I'll just have to instruct Frosh on what to do differently and then watch the changing acceptance letter on my wall.

Yes! This time, I am not going to let some boy distract me from making something of myself. No way. This time, I'm not going to let a guy who's going to dump me anyway ruin my future. This time, I'm going to focus on school and get into a great college.

This time I have a plan.

I call Frosh immediately. "Guess where you're going."

"Can I pee first? I just got home two seconds ago."

"The important thing is that you're home. 'Cause you have work to do. You're going to UCLA!"

"You mean for the weekend? To visit Maya?"

I laugh. "No, silly dilly. I mean later on. In four years."

"I am?"

"Yes! You are. You are going to change our life, for the better. Before me, you didn't care about school. You didn't value your friends."

"I do too—"

"You didn't value them *enough*. Bryan came along and took you under his wing. Sure, he carried you at first, but then he dropped you into a big pile of mud. So I am here to steer you. To tell you what you need. To save you. Not only are you ridding your life of Bryan and keeping your friends, you're going to get us into a decent college. UCLA, maybe." I can see it clearly. The new me. Laughing with my girlfriends. Going off to a great school, my sun-drenched hair blowing in the California wind. Carefree, happy, supersmart me.

"What school am I supposed to go to? I mean, what school did you get into?"

"That's the thing. You were supposed to go to Stulen."

"Stupid State," she says in disbelief. "All you could get into was Stupid State? What did you do, fail junior year?"

"No, I didn't *fail*. I just didn't *try*. I didn't care about college. I just wanted to be with Bryan and he didn't care about college either—or so he claimed—and we thought we would just save money and . . . never mind. It's over. The point is that as of today, I've been accepted to Ballor."

"Is that good?"

"It's like half a step above Stulen. But you're going to get us into a better school. A superb school. If Maya can do it, why can't we?"

She's silent for a moment and then she laughs. " 'Cause Maya got all the brains."

"Don't say that! That's a terrible thing to say. You're smart. I'm smart. And anything is possible, no? If I can talk to myself in the past, surely I can get myself into UCLA!"

"Okay, smarty-pants, so how are we going to get into UCLA exactly?"

"Let's see," I say, thinking. "Maya had an A average."

"You think I can get that too?" she asks. "I didn't even have an A average in middle school."

"It'll take a lot of work. But you can do it. What are your courses again?"

"English, algebra, American history, economics, chemistry, French, and . . . I'm forgetting something. Oh, gym."

"Okay. Let's think this through. Your problem in English is that you don't always finish the book in time. That's the trick. Read the book before class. If you do, you'll get a lot more out of it and then you'll be able to ace your essays."

"Of course I can do that. I'm reading *Jane Eyre* right now. Why wouldn't I finish the book? I like to read."

"You do? Oh yeah, you do. But you like hanging out with your boyfriend more. But now you'll finish it tonight after we get off the phone," I order.

"Tonight? But we're going to Karin's and—"

"No time for Karin," I say. "You have work to do!"

"But—"

"No buts, Frosh! Do you want this to work or not?" When she doesn't say anything, I continue. "Next. Algebra. This one's easy. Pay attention! And if you don't understand a concept, go to peer tutoring. If you understand what's going on in class, then you'll do fine on the tests. Next."

"American history."

"Right! That's no problem. Did Karin tape all her classes back then?"

"Yup. Every one."

"She still does it. She's in my world history class this year. Not that we sit together. I mean, we didn't used to when Bryan and I—" I clear my throat. "Everything's fine now. You stopped studying with Karin when you started spending so much time with Bryan, but that won't be a problem anymore, so you're good. And it's the same idea as algebra—if you understand the concepts, you'll ace it. Don't just try to memorize the dates. Next."

"Economics."

"All you have to do is read the chapters he assigns. The quizzes and tests are right out of the book. Next?"

"Chemistry."

"Easy peasy. Tash will help you. She's going to study premed at Brown, you know."

"She is? That is so awesome! Tell me more! What about Karin and Joelle? Where are they going?"

"From what I heard around school, Joelle's going to FIT—"

"That's fantastic. Does she still wear the coolest outfits ever?"

"Yup. She makes most of her own clothes now."

"Wow. And what about Karin?"

"Karin's going to Buff State, from what I heard. It hasn't come up in conversation, though, so I'm assuming it's the same."

"Cool. Yay for them."

Yes, yay for them. They've moved on in their lives. Everyone has moved on. Time for me to play catch-up and move on too. I'm moving on all the way to UCLA! "Now, where were we?"

"French."

"Hmmm," I murmur. "That's a tough one. No one speaks any French except . . ." Except Bryan. Having lived in Montreal, he's bilingual. Bryan used to talk to me in French when he was trying to be cute. But I'm not going to Bryan for help. Not this time. Not ever. "You're just going to have to focus. And do your homework."

"Do my homework. Got it."

"You're writing all this down, right?" I ask.

"Where?"

"In your notebook! Remember?"

"Yup."

I open my desk drawer, pull out the green notebook to see if she's really writing it down. Nope. "Liar."

"Hold on." She sighs. I hear her scrambling to find it. The words appear on the page. "Done. Next?"

"Gym. Who do you have again? Zetner?"

"Yeah."

"That's not too hard. You don't get an A, but if I remember correctly, you don't do too badly. It's not like you have homework."

"So what do I do, then? Nothing?"

"Just try harder. You don't put much effort in. If you try a little, I bet you could get an A."

"Will try in gym. Next?"

"SATs. Maya scored in the ninety-eighth percentile."

"That sounds super high. What was your percentile?"

My cheeks get hot. "Not ninety-eight."

"So I need to have a good GPA and a high score. Fabo. Can I worry about my SATs when I'm a junior, then?"

"Do Olympic athletes start training the year before they compete? Absolutely not. You need to start preparing now." As I say this, my dad passes by my door—still in his bathrobe. Does he ever get dressed?

She really is going to have to focus on those SAT scores. Like Maya, I'm going to need a scholarship if I want to go to some fancy college. My parents can definitely *not* afford it.

"How do I do that exactly?" she asks, bringing me back to the present. Or the present-past. Whatever.

Hmmm. "Your weak spot was really the verbal. You know, those crazy words. Like 'coagulate.' "

"What does that mean?"

"Exactly my point. Maybe if we start now, you'll be a verbal genius." If she memorizes one word a day, she could have the vocabulary of an English professor in time for the SATs. "Yes! Superb idea!"

"What is?" she asks nervously.

"Memorizing one SAT word a day. By the time you're a junior, you'll know the entire dictionary."

"Starting when?"

"Today, of course. With 'coagulate.' "

"What does it mean?"

"One sec," I say, and go into Maya's old room. On her

bookshelf are about twenty SAT-prep books—none of which I ever opened. "According to my SparkNotes SAT-prep book, it means 'to thicken, clot.' "

"Can you use it in a sentence?"

"The orange juice left in my glass has coagulated into a crusty mess."

"That's gross."

"Yeah, well, I'm not going to drink it." I sit down on Maya's old bed and flip through the book. Why didn't I even bother studying the first time around? I remember the day of the test, the burst of hope I felt that maybe I could ace this without any prep. I'd surprise everyone. Surprise myself. "Did you write that down?" I ask her.

"Yup," she says, and I hear her scribbling.

"Now back to us. And getting into UCLA. It's not just about getting A's."

"It's not?"

"No," I say with disgust. My little rudderless vessel doesn't know anything. "You're going to be busy."

"What should I do?"

"Stuff. You need to do stuff."

"Can you be more specific?"

"Yes. You need a well-rounded resume. To get into a good college, you need to do some extracurriculars."

"What do Karin, Joelle, and Tash do? As seniors, I mean."

"Let's see. Karin was a gymnast, but apparently she's now a cheerleader with a nose job— "

"Sorry about that," she says sheepishly. "But it's better

than an eating disorder. And I'm going to come up with a plan to help her."

"No plans without consulting me," I remind her. "Tash is in some of the science clubs."

"Do they have boyfriends?"

"Karin does. A guy named Stevey she met at the mall. He goes to Florence East. He's very cute. He's his school's top swimmer or something. But I don't think Tash has gone out with anyone."

"Really? No one? That's sad. Is she still shy?"

"Yeah. She never talks about guys she likes. She's focused on school. It's not easy to get into Brown, you know."

"And what about Joelle?" she asks.

"She's yearbook editor," I tell her.

"Oh, she just joined the staff this week! That's so exciting. Any boyfriends?"

"She was with Jerome Cohen for a few months freshman year. But that's all I know about."

"Really? She is? I mean, she was? That's so cool! She has a crush on him!"

"I remember," I say. "I think we help fix them up." As the words leave my mouth, I wonder if maybe from now on I shouldn't be telling her so much about the future. In case the future ends up like Karin's nose—under construction.

"Oh, fun! How?"

It's not going to happen like it did before anyway. I guess I can tell. "He asks Bryan to ask me if she likes him. Who knows? Maybe without me and Bryan they don't go out."

"What? That's so sad! She really likes him! I don't want

her not to get to go out with Jerome just because Bryan cheated on us. That's so unfair."

Right. Well. "We don't know for sure they don't go out. Maybe he asks someone else for the details. Let me find out if anything's changed before we feel bad, okay?" Next time I'm keeping my mouth shut.

"Fine," she says.

"Now back to you. You need some extracurriculars. Wanna try out for cheerleading too?"

"No. First of all, I am not so cheery. Or flexible. Second, the tryouts were today. I missed them. And I don't want to end up with a nose job too."

I spread my legs into a V and struggle to open them all the way. "Can you do the splits?"

"Um, no. Can you?"

"No! But I used to be able to. You sure you can't? Try."

She groans. "I really don't think I—"

"Just try!"

I hear shuffling and then an "Ow!"

"No. I can't," she says.

"We used to be able to do them."

"When we were six."

"Still!" I say. "What happened to us? Six-year-old us could do it. I bet if six-year-old us did it every day, then we would still be able to do it."

"Then call six-year-old us," she grumbles.

I pause. "I would if I could."

"What other extracurriculars can I do?" she asks. "Ones that don't involve turning my body into a pretzel."

"What about yearbook?"

"Sounds boring."

"No, it'll be like making a scrapbook."

"I make scrapbooks?"

I made one. Once upon a time. In a world that no longer exists. "You could work with Joelle," I say instead.

"I guess. I think sign-up was last week, though."

"Trust me, they won't mind if you join. It's yearbook. There aren't exactly tryouts to get in."

"I think Joelle has a yearbook lunch meeting tomorrow."

"Perfect! You'll go too."

"Good. Is that enough?"

"For today! Quick—coagulate! Use it in a sentence!"

She clears her throat. "My brain is beginning to coagulate."

chapter sixteen

Tuesday, September 13 • • • Freshman Year

When the lunch bell rings, I call to Joelle, "Are you going to yearbook?"

"Yup." She breaks into a big smile. "Why, wanna come?"

"I was thinking about it." Translation: Ivy is forcing me to do this.

She is also making me try out for the school play, *Beauty and the Beast,* in which I will most likely be cast as a dinner plate, since I have no talent.

"Fabo!" She clutches a silver folder marked *Yearbook* under her arm. "What made you change your mind?"

"Oh, you know," I say. "College applications."

She bursts out laughing. "Seriously? You're thinking about those now? In the first month of high school?"

I guess it does sound kind of insane. I shrug. "Never hurts to plan ahead."

She puts her arm around my shoulders. "I didn't know you were such a go-getter."

Me neither. "Where's the meeting?"

"In the basement," she says.

I didn't know there was a basement. At the end of the hall, Joelle and I walk down the steps. Between the school newspaper office and the French club is the yearbook room. It is a square concrete room that houses a few computers and a lunch table–sized desk. There are about ten of us here, mostly sophomores. Joelle and I go to the back of the room.

"So, do you want to be yearbook editor someday or something?" she asks, flipping her hair.

"What, me? No. You're going to be—" I stop myself in midsentence. She does not know yet that she's going to be yearbook editor, so I probably shouldn't tell her.

"I'm going to be what?"

I point to her folder. "You're going to be the best yearbook staffer ever."

"Yeah," she says with a smile. "That goes without saying."

"Will you show me what I have to do?" Or maybe I should just save time and ask my future self what I already did. Kidding.

"Joy will tell us," she says.

Joy, the tiny blond senior sitting on the teacher's desk, waves. "Hey, thanks for coming!"

"My pleasure," I say.

"Why don't you guys start by looking through old yearbooks to get ideas for some page spreads. Also, if anyone has any fund-raising ideas, let me know ASAP. We are poor, people, and we need to reach out."

"Sounds good," I say, and she hands us the last five years of books.

We dig right in. Most are divided up the same way—faculty, then a few pages for each grade, then about forty pages for the seniors. Each graduating student gets a quarter of a page to write his or her statement. Most of them are made up of quotes and sayings, like "Carpe Diem," and song lyrics from "Lost in the Wind," and cagey messages to friends, like "candle nightx8" and "GH—thankx4thePurple." Or Erika Pallick's five-year-old declaration to MX: "1st truelove. URevrything2me." Or Lisa Viergo's "To Kayla, my BFF. Thnx4lovngMeSoMch & NoingMebttr thn I no myself."

I wonder what happened to Erika and MX. Does he still mean everything to her? Did they go to college together? And are Lisa and Kayla still best friends? Or did they lose touch when they went to college?

"Any great ideas?" Joy asks, crouching beside us.

"I wish we could do a follow-up on some of these people. See what happened to them," I say.

Joy cocks her head to the side. "Can't you just search for them on Google?"

"Yeah," I admit. "But then I feel like I'm stalking them. And it would be cool to have it in print."

Joelle taps her fingers against a book from last year. "If we include one page of Where Are They Nows, we could start selling alumni the books. As a keepsake. And maybe even get some of them to make donations."

"Exactly," I say.

"I love it!" Joy tells us, clapping her hands. "You two are going to be my rock stars. I can tell. I'll get you guys an alumni list and you can start e-mailing to see who has news. That's definitely a page worth doing."

"Fabo," I say, squeezing Joelle's arm. Yearbook committee is pretty awesome. Who knew?

I flip back through the senior statements. I can't wait to write mine. Who knows what—or who—I'll be sad to leave behind? I guess I can always ask Ivy. The bell rings, and I slam closed the yearbook. Kind of takes the fun out of it, though.

chapter seventeen

Tuesday, May 27 • • • Senior Year

"Hey," I say, sliding into the empty desk beside Karin in world history.

"Hi," she says, forehead wrinkling. "What's up?"

I plop my pencil case onto the desk. "Not too much. You?"

"Nothing . . . do you have something to tell me?"

"Um . . . no? Should I?"

"Then why are you here?"

"Why am I in world history?"

She wraps a ringlet around her index finger. "Yeah. Shouldn't you be in Draker's AP world history right now?"

Huh? Oh! "Yes!" I say, bolting up and grabbing my books. "Of course I should be. I just wanted to ask you . . . what you were doing after school. Wanna come over?"

"Sure," she says, waving. "See you at lunch!"

My head spinning, I run back to my locker. It's weird

how no one else seems freaked out by the instant changes in my world. For everyone else it's just a normal day. Karin used to have world history with her former best friend. Then she had it with her best friend. Then her best friend was in AP history. La, la, la. She used to have a crooked nose. No more. La, la, la, la.

I stare at my class schedule, which is taped to the inside of my locker. I used to be in regular classes. Now? All AP. La, la, la, la, la.

Sure, it's confusing, but . . . well done, Frosh! It's a good thing AP exams were two weeks ago, or I would be in serious trouble. But post-exam classes are the best. We watched *Romeo and Juliet* in AP English.

I'm walking on cloud eleven right until lunch, when I spot Celia and Bryan.

Kissing. In the middle of the hallway. Their arms around each other. Her hands on his back.

"Ugh," I say, looking away. I hope their saliva coagulates and chokes them. I like her better when she's insulting people.

"What's wrong?" Karin asks.

"I'm a little nauseated."

" 'Cause of Bryan and Celia's PDA? Me too."

"You don't still like him, do you?" I ask. I don't think I can deal with that.

"Noooooo. I'm crazy about Stevey."

"Thank God. I mean—good." I pat her shoulder. "Um, how long have they been going out again?" I motion to the vile couple with my chin.

"Hmmm, maybe since February?"

Only three months. Take that, Celia. They don't have what we had.

"There's no way it will last," Karin adds. "He's such a player."

Now I really stop in my tracks. What? He is? How did *that* happen? I smile to myself. So does that mean the only girl he could have a four-year relationship with was me?

As we pass them in the hall, Celia's hand lowers to the top of his jeans, and the smile is quickly wiped off my face. Slutbag.

"So, tell me about prom," I say. In other words, do I have a date?

"What about it?"

Must tread carefully. "Remind me what the plans are?"

"The limo is going to pick Stevey and me up first, and then we're going to get you and Harry, and then we'll pick up Tash and then Joelle."

Me and Harry. I'm going to prom with Harry Travis. Insane. There will be no kissing though. I don't want a face rash in my prom pics.

We pick up two trays of cheese ravioli (at least Karin's eating!) and sit down at our table beside Tash, who's already deep into a chicken salad.

"What's up, ladies?" she asks.

"Just discussing prom plans," I tell her.

"Can't wait," she says, rolling her eyes. "I can't believe you guys are making me go."

Karin elbows her in the side. "Of course we're making you go!"

"Yeah," I add. "It'll be fun. Karin, Stevey, you and Joelle, me and . . . Harry." Me and Harry!

"I don't know why you won't let me find you a date," Karin tells Tash. "It could be fun."

"I don't want to be forced to spend the night making small talk with some random person," Tash says, shaking her head.

"But random boys can be fun," Karin says, looking around the room. "And the cute ones look good in pictures."

Let's hope.

Karin subtly lifts her chin toward a guy in the corner. "What about Nick Dennings? You have a few AP classes with him, right? You guys could talk science experiments. Plus, he could probably take you in a stretch limo."

Nick Dennings's mom sold her Internet business for a gazillion dollars last year. Plus his acne cleared up over the summer. He went from Not to Hot overnight.

Tash shakes her head. "He's taking his girlfriend. Some sophomore."

"Never mind, then." Karin keeps looking. "Jonah Stoller?"

"His tongue ring gives me the creeps."

I can play this game too! "What about . . ." I spot Sean Puttin in the lunch line. "Sean Puttin! He's pretty cute if you like the Connecticut look."

Karin drops her fork into her ravioli. "Are you kidding me?"

"Why?" I ask. "What's the problem?"

Tash looks intently at my face and laughs. "It's like you have amnesia or something."

"Right. Amnesia. Ha-ha." I squirm in my seat.

"He's an ass," Karin says. "We hate him."

"Of course we do!" I laugh nervously. "Why do we hate him again?"

"Because of what he said," Tash explains, "about you."

I put down my fork. "What did he say about me?"

"You seriously don't remember?" Karin asks in amazement.

"I do, I do . . . it's just . . ." I need to come up with an explanation for my severe memory lapses. Pronto. "It's just that I was . . . in a car accident."

"What?" they scream.

"When?" Karin asks, putting her arm around my shoulders, concern etched all over her face.

"Over the weekend," I continue. "I'm fine, but I hit my head. And the doctor said that I may experience some memory issues. For a few days."

"Why didn't you tell us?" Karin asks.

"I didn't want to worry you," I say, looking down at my hands. I can't believe they're buying this. But I guess it sounds more plausible than time travel. "But anyway, I'm going to be fine. You'll just have to indulge me and fill in the blanks for a bit. Like with Sean Puttin. What happened again?"

Tash shrugs. "Maybe some things are better blocked out."

"I have some things I'd like to block out," Karin says.

"Did I tell you that I saw my mom and dad doing it last week?"

"Yes," Tash says. "You've told us multiple times. And now I can't block it out either."

"Please spill it," I beg.

Karin hesitates. "It was about your kissing technique."

"What's wrong with my kissing technique?" Bryan had no issues with my kissing technique. At least, he never said anything about my kissing technique.

She hesitates again. "He said you kiss like a fish."

Jaw drops. "He said what? How does he even know what I kiss like?"

Karin and Tash give each other a Devi's-an-alien look. "Because you kissed him. Last year. Have you blocked that out too?"

Yes. Apparently I have. What does a fish even kiss like? Fish don't kiss. Sean Puttin is a preppy moron! I do *not* kiss like a fish. Unless that's why Bryan broke up with me. Because I kiss like a fish.

I look up. Karin and Tash are both staring at me.

I guess I should say something. "Forget Sean, then. We definitely don't want him in our limo." I send a quick text to Frosh: Do not kiss Sean Puttin. And beware of Harry's beard! It hurts! xo Ivy

"Forget me having a date," Tash says, going back to her chicken salad. "Joelle doesn't have one, so what do I need one for?"

Didn't Joelle mention in the car the other day something about waiting for Jerome Cohen to ask her? And

aren't I supposed to find out what happened with Jerome
Cohen anyway? "Any chance Jerome Cohen asks her?" I
ask, hoping that they won't give me another Devi's-insane
look.

They give me another Devi's-insane look.

Tash snorts. "If Joelle mentions Jerome Cohen one more
time, I may have to strangle her."

Karin nods. "She really needs to get over him."

Aha! So they did go out. "They went out so long ago . . .
when we were freshmen, right?" I hope that's still true.

"Yes," Tash grumbles. "A million years ago."

"And she's still hung up on him," I say. I think I'm getting it.

Tash rolls her eyes. "You think?"

"She should have said yes to Kellerman," Karin says.
"He would have made a decent prom date. As long as he
changed out of his sweatpants. Do you think he even owns
a pair of jeans?"

"No, she'd prefer to remain uncommitted on the zero
chance that Jerome asks her." Tash shakes her head. "I bet
he's not even going. Hipsters like Jerome don't go to prom."

I look around the room. "Where is Joelle, anyway?"

Tash takes another forkful of her salad. "Yearbook, I
think. Hey, shouldn't you be there too?"

"Should I?" I ask.

Karin laughs. "Aren't you the coeditor?"

"Try it on for me!" Karin says, lying across my bed. "What color is it again?"

"Red," I say, and open my closet.

"Really? I thought you hated red."

"I do but—" Bryan thought red was sexy. Never mind. The dress that stares up at me from my closet is not red. It's silver, ankle-length, and drapey. Cinderella-y but without the puff. Wow. It's perfect. "I forgot. My dress is silver." I giggle weirdly.

"Your memory is seriously whacked. But I love the dress. Is it Izzy Simpson?"

I peek at the tag. "Knockoff. It's from Raffles."

"Good find."

I dump my clothes onto the floor and slip on the new dress.

Karin zips up the back and I give her a twirl.

"Wow. You look amazing. Seriously."

I admire my reflection in the mirror. It does look pretty good. What was I thinking with red? I must have been crazy.

"What shoes did you get?" she asks.

Good question. I rifle through my closet. I see my red prom heels. But no silver ones. How did that happen? That's not going to look right. "I think I still need a pair," I say.

"Only a week and a half left to go. We should go shopping this week. Are you going to get four-inches?"

"Are you crazy? Why would I do that? I won't be able to walk."

"Isn't Tom like six foot three?"

Huh? "Tom? Who's Tom?"

Her forehead crinkles with concern. "Your amnesia is acting up again. Tom Kradowski? Your prom date?"

My what? What happened? "Right . . . Tom Kradowski." Apparently Frosh did something and I have a new prom date. What happened to Harry? Harry is hot! I catch my reflection again and see that I no longer have a chin rash. Does this mean that I no longer made out with Harry on Friday? Did the beard warning throw Frosh off?

I barely know Tom Kradowski! I don't think I've ever said two words to him. But I must have, right? At least to ask him to prom or to accept his invitation. At the moment, all I know about Tom is that he's very tall. Like six foot three. Kind of reminds me of a giraffe. Boooooo. I want Hot Harry back! "I guess I will need higher heels."

"Unless you're wearing stilettos, you're still going to spend most of the night looking up."

After changing back into my clothes, I sit at the opposite end of my bed and glance at my bulletin board. *Congratulations on your acceptance to Hofstra!*

New prom date, new school . . . pretty soon I'll be an entirely brand-new me.

chapter eighteen

Tuesday, September 13 • • • Freshman Year

"Still doing homework?" Mom asks me. My work is spread across the kitchen table.

"Yup," I say, stifling a yawn.

"It's after ten. Shouldn't you get to bed?"

"Soon," I tell her, wondering why Ivy hasn't called to check in. "I just have to finish reading a chapter for economics. We have a quiz tomorrow."

"You've been at it for hours," she says. "I've never seen you work so hard."

Because I've never worked so hard.

"I know high school can be overwhelming, but you don't want to overdo it," she tells me.

Even though everyone was going to the mall after school, I came home to study. Sure, I'm not ditching my friends for Bryan—I'm ditching them for homework. I didn't want to—but I did it. Because that's what Ivy told me to do. But if she doesn't even bother to call—even though I sent two texts—then I'm not going to listen to her anymore.

"Thanks for helping me with my song for the play tryouts," I tell her.

"No problem. I used to help Maya all the time. And you're going to do great tomorrow."

Moms are the most unbiased judges, aren't they? I'm singing "Kiss the Girl" from *The Little Mermaid*. Since the play is *Beauty and the Beast,* I figure I might as well stay in the Disney family for the tryouts.

Ivy finally calls a half hour later.

"Where have you been?" I ask bitterly. I close my textbooks with a bang. "I've been waiting."

"Karin was over," Ivy says.

"She was? Glad you get to hang out with friends while I have to work."

"I had to work during lunch, thank you very much. Yearbook meeting."

I cradle the phone between my ear and shoulder and carry my work up the stairs. "You're still on yearbook! Fabo! Isn't it fun? It's a lot of work, going through all those photos and page layouts, but still fun."

"I wouldn't know—I don't remember doing any of it! But I must have, huh? Our page proofs are already in. We had a celebratory pizza party with the surplus from our ad sales and alumni pages. You would not believe how much former students give to get their names listed in the Where Are They Now section."

I'm too annoyed at her to be happy about my alumni idea still being around three years later. "So you have pizza parties and hang out with my friends while I study and practice singing 'Kiss the Girl' again and again until I sound like a scratched CD."

She laughs. "I guess. But it's working, no? We got into Hofstra and I'm yearbook editor."

Huh? "You are? I thought Joelle was yearbook editor." Oh, no. "Don't tell me I stole her job!"

"Relax. We're coeditors. You didn't usurp her."

I dump my books onto my desk. "*Unsurp?*"

"No. 'Usurp.' Your SAT word for today, my little friend. It means 'to seize by force, take possession of without right.' "

Sounds like a brand of slushy. "Got it. Usurp."

"Can you use it in a sentence?"

Ivy is usurping all my fun. "I'd feel really badly if I *usurped* Joelle's position."

"Bad," she says. "You'd feel bad. I think. I don't know. Whatever. But let's not forget about the essay portion of the SATs. You can't sound illiterate. And what's 'coagulate'?"

"To thicken," I say, on autopilot.

"Very good. You're doing wonderfully. You're obviously doing well in your classes."

"I definitely understood what was going on in algebra," I say. "And Karin said I could come over whenever I want and listen to her tapes. And Tash said she'd explain to me what was going on in chemistry tomorrow at lunch."

"Cool! All you need is a few more activities and we'll be there."

I close my eyes. "More activities? Are you kidding?"

"I know, I know, I'm sorry. You must be overwhelmed, but . . . it's the best thing for us. I swear."

"Ivy, I don't know how much more I can do. Between yearbook and memorizing stuff for the play and keeping up with my schoolwork, I'm going to have a lot on my plate. Omigod, I missed the premiere of *TTYL!*" How did I forget about my favorite show?

"I can tell you what happens," she says. "They all—"

"No spoilers!" I scream, covering my ears and dropping the phone onto the carpet. Whoops. "I'm only picking up if you promise not to tell me what happens!" I loosen my hands.

I hear her muffled promise and pick up the phone again.

"They all die," she says.

Ahhhh! "I'm going to kill you."

"I'm kidding, I'm kidding. They don't die. They get into a car accident and suffer from short-term amnesia." She giggles.

"That would never happen on *TTYL!* That's way too hokey."

She giggles again. "You'd think. But I'm kidding with you. Honestly, I don't even watch the show anymore, so I have no idea what's going on."

I breathe a sigh of relief. "Good. Let's keep it that way."

"Back to the real world. Colleges like applicants who are well rounded. I think you need a sport."

That does not sound fun. "Can we talk about it tomorrow? I'm really tired." I yawn. Loudly.

"It's only ten-thirty!"

"That's late! It's a school night!"

She laughs. "You're so dimples."

I sigh and plant my head smack in the middle of my pillow. "What does that even mean?"

"Oh, it's just an expression we use—I use—to mean cute. Forget it."

"Will do." I close my eyes. My eyelids are extra-heavy. "So can I go to bed now? Anything else?"

"Yes, actually. One more. I know that I'm asking a lot, but I was thinking you should do some volunteer work."

"You mean we should try our Save the World list again."

"I meant more like licking envelopes for the Red Cross. Something to add to your application. Something small, no? I still think we need to fix all the stuff on the list eventually, but the plastic surgery thing still freaks me out. I don't want to make anything worse."

"Yeah. I get it."

"We should probably get you all settled first, anyway. Before trying the big stuff, no? Safer to use ourselves as the test dummy until we've gotten all the wrinkles out."

I sigh. "Good point." I guess saving the world can wait a few more days. It's not like time is something we're running out of. In fact, I kinda think we have too much of it. "So, how come you say 'no' after all your sentences?"

"I do not!"

"You do too. You just said, 'Before trying the big stuff, no?' "

"I don't know what you're talking about," she huffs.

Whatever. I yawn again. "Anything else?"

"Yes! Did you get my text today?"

"About Harry's beard? Yeah. Why would he grow a beard? Gross."

"Just forget I said anything, 'kay? What about the Sean part?"

"Not kissing him? Yes, I got it." Was I planning on kissing Sean Puttin? No, I was not. Although he is kind of cute.

"Good. He tells everyone you kiss like a fish."

I nibble on my lip. "Why?"

"Because he's a jerk-face."

"Why do I kiss him if he's a jerk-face, then?"

"I don't know. I don't even remember it happening. But if I were you, which I am, I would not kiss him in the first place. Did you write it down in the notebook?"

I'm pretty sure that's something I'll remember, but I climb out of bed, turn my light back on, find my spiral notebook, and open it. Then I write DO NOT KISS SEAN PUTTIN. "Done," I say. Then I add, "I don't kiss like a fish, do I?"

"Of course not!" she huffs. "You're a superb kisser."

"Swear?" I ask nervously.

"Of course. I bet he kisses like a fish, and you were trying to compensate."

"I have no idea how I kiss," I admit. "I've never kissed anyone."

"That's right. You still haven't had your first kiss!"

"Thanks for rubbing it in."

"I'm not. It's dimp—sweet."

I hug my pillow to my chest. "When do I have my first kiss? Real kiss, I mean. Not like with Jarred and Anthony. With tongue."

She laughs. "You're seriously adorable."

"Don't laugh!" I say, my cheeks burning. "Just tell me the truth. What's my first *real* kiss like?" I know what I want my first kiss to be like. How I imagine it being. Sweet and soft and romantic with someone who makes me feel like the luckiest girl in the world.

"Oh. Well. I don't know."

What is she talking about? "How do you not know? You're me in the future! You must have had a first kiss."

"Yeah. Lucky for you I'm not Maya."

I giggle, but then I feel bad. I miss my sister. "She's in college now. I'm sure she's kissed someone." I've been so busy with Ivy, I kind of forgot about her. Her role has been *usurped*.

"How would I know? It's not like we talk about stuff like that."

"But what about *my* first kiss?"

"I remember what happened to me, Frosh," she says softly. "But what is going to happen with you is not the same as what happened with me. Get it?"

Aha. "Your first kiss was with Bryan." Obviously.

She doesn't say anything.

"Ivy? Are you still there?"

"Yeah. I am. And it was."

"So I guess you don't know who my first kiss is with, then. Since it'll be different than yours."

"Yours will be different," she repeats, and her voice sounds faint or something. "I have to go."

"Good night," I say. But she has already hung up.

chapter nineteen

Tuesday, May 27 • • • Senior Year

Even if she'll never experience it, I can't stop remembering.

The first kiss.

It wasn't after movie-turned-bowling night. Or three days later, Tuesday—Frosh's today—on our first Subway lunch. It was that Friday night, September sixteenth. I invited him over. I tried on about nine cute-yet-casual outfits before settling on jeans and a stretch V-neck shirt that showed off both my eyes and my boobs. I painted my fingernails and toenails soft pink. After an extra-long gel-and-scrunch routine, I tied my hair back in a ponytail to give it a more chill look. I did my makeup extra light to look natural, and brushed my teeth about seven times just in case.

Dad was working, but Mom made us peanut butter and white chocolate cookies and then disappeared into her room. Bryan was sitting next to me on the couch. Of course

I couldn't concentrate on TV. How could I when the cutest boy in the history of the world was sitting right beside me? When the credits rolled, he asked me if I wanted to go for a walk.

"Where to?" I asked.

"Hedgemonds Park?" he said. "We'll rank their swings on a scale of one to ten."

I slipped into my favorite black sandals. It was one of those perfect Florence September nights. Warm, breezy, clear stars sprinkled across the sky.

We sat beside each other on the swings. Pushing back and forth and back and forth. He started showing off, pushing higher and higher. I pushed higher and higher.

My sandal flew off.

He started laughing and jumped off the swing to get it.

He picked it up and I thought he was going to make a whole Cinderella production of it, but instead, he just stood by my swing until I slowed to a halt.

Of course I knew what was coming.

He put his hands over mine and leaned down and kissed me.

His lips were soft and light and sweet and everything else disappeared except for the kiss and the moment. The perfect kiss in that perfect moment.

Everything I had ever wanted, imagined. Happening to me. Happened to me. And now . . .

If you kiss a boy and he doesn't remember, did it really happen?

If it didn't happen, why do the memories still hurt?

chapter twenty

Wednesday, September 14 • • • Freshman Year

I'm practicing my lines in my head when I run smack into Bryan. And I mean *smack* into. He's standing in the hall. I'm not paying attention. I walk into him. My books scatter into the air like pigeons under attack.

"You need to be declared a national disaster area," he says with a laugh.

"Tell me about it," I say, feeling my cheeks burn. "It's my fault. I was trying to do two things at once."

He bends down to help me collect my stuff. "What's that? Walking and breathing?"

I giggle. "No, smarty-pants, walking and practicing my lines for the play." I pick up my economics quiz. Mr. Jacobs handed them back right away and I got an A! I am an economics genius. But now's no time to gloat . . . adorable Bryan is talking to me!

"Oh, you're a play girl," he says.

"When you say it like that, it sounds kind of naughty," I say with another giggle. Omigod. What am I doing? I'm flirting with him! I can't flirt with him. No flirting with Bryan allowed! Even if he's adorable. Even if I'm all flushed.

His smile shows off his perfect dimples. "You strike me as more nice than naughty."

"Is that a compliment or an insult?" I ask.

"A compliment."

I pile the last book into my arms and look right at him. Shoot. Why's he still so cute?

"How's the boyfriend?" he asks.

I'm about to say "The what?" But then I remember my lie. "Oh, he's fine."

"What's his name again?"

"Um, his name?" What is his name? "It's . . . um . . . Ivy." Ah! "Ivan."

He nods as though I didn't just sound like an idiot. "What school does he go to?"

"Oh, he doesn't go to school here. He lives . . . not far. In Buffalo."

"Do you get to see each other a lot?"

"No. But we talk a lot." I wave my cell phone. "Free long distance."

He gives me another one of his dimpled smiles. Adorable. Wait a sec! Is that where Ivy got the expression "dimples"? Because Bryan's are so cute?

"Good luck," he says.

Huh? "With my boyfriend?"

He laughs again. "With the auditions."

Right. "Thanks. See you later." I give him a brief salute and then hurry on my way.

Karin's locker is diagonal from mine, and Joelle and Tash are already waiting for us.

Joelle is dancing. "What are you ladies doing now? Anyone wanna come over?"

"I have practice," Karin says with a big smile. "Sorry!"

Yes, Karin made cheerleading. Not that I'm surprised, since I already knew she would. They posted the list at lunch. I've thought about trying to get her to quit, but I'm not sure what I should tell her. Get out now before you become obsessed with plastic surgery? But then what if she gets another eating disorder? Or becomes obsessed with tattoos? Or becomes a drug addict? It's like Ivy said—trying to fix one thing can lead to unintended consequences. I've decided to try a subtler approach.

"I can't come either. I have play tryouts," I say to Joelle. Then I turn back to Karin and add, "Before you go, I just want to mention—you look fabo today."

"Thanks," she says, smiling.

"Really," I tell her. "Your boobs look terrific in that shirt."

She blushes and fidgets with her top. "Um, thanks?"

Joelle bursts out laughing.

"Doesn't she?" I ask the other girls. "I wish I had her boobs." My plan is to layer on the boob praise for the next three and a half years.

Tash is the same color as Karin.

Joelle puts her hand on her hip. "Let's see . . . yes, she does have good boobs."

"Both of you wear the same cup size as I do," Karin says.

"Maybe," I say. "But yours are the perfect shape."

Joelle sticks her chest out. "Are you saying mine are shaped imperfectly?"

"You also have perfectly shaped boobs," I say. Must be careful. I don't want to drive her to the knife too.

"Why, thank you," Joelle says.

"Can we get back to talking about the play?" Karin asks. "You guys are freaking me out."

"Yes, the play," Joelle says. "Did I tell you I'm helping with costumes and design? Maybe I'll get to dress you as Belle."

I laugh. "Don't count on it. I have no talent. I'm more of a background-teacup sort of girl."

Joelle stops dancing and turns to Tash. "Why don't you audition too?"

Tash almost drops her books. "Are you kidding?"

"No, I'm a hundred percent serious."

Tash shakes her head. "I'm not really a play person."

"Neither am I," I say. "You should do it." As soon as I say the words, though, I try to swallow them back. Must not encourage friends to do random things that could change the course of their lives. Who knows what dangerous path the school play could lead her on? Whatever. She's not going to audition. At the library during lunch, while she helped me with chemistry, I told her I was trying out, and she showed no interest in the play whatsoever.

Joelle squeezes Tash's shoulder. "Don't you want to get into a good premed program? Maybe this could help."

You already get into Brown, I want to tell her, but I don't. That would be weird.

"It would be good for you," Joelle annoyingly continues. "Help you break out of your shell. Come on. If Devi can do it, so can you."

Tash switches her schoolbag to her other shoulder. I expect her to say no way. To say she's not interested. To say thanks but no thanks. She shrugs. "All right."

Huh?

"Good for you!" Joelle sings, clapping her on the back.

Not good! Ivy is going to kill me! Tash's future is fine. Her future is *great*. She's going to Brown! She's studying medicine! She wants to cure cancer! I can't let her try out for the play. It could ruin everything. "No, no, no!" I wail.

They all stare at me.

Tash blinks. "You don't want me to try out?"

"No. I mean, yes. Um, of course I do. But you don't have the script. You know. For the audition. You should have told me at lunch if you wanted to try out and then you could have had time to study it, but at this point . . ." I shake my head.

"What do I have to do?" she asks.

"You have to be able to read from the script. You know. To act it out. The auditions are now. You're not going to have time to memorize it. And also, you need to prepare a song."

"Her memory is pretty photographic," Joelle says. "And can't she just sing 'Happy Birthday'? That's a song, right?"

"Happy Birthday"! Why didn't I think of that? I

wouldn't have had to practice my song a million times and broken all the mirrors in my house. "You're going to sing?" I ask her. "In public?"

Tash shrinks into herself. "I don't know . . . "

"Oh, shut up," Joelle says. "You're doing it. I dare you. And Devi will be right next to you. And I'm coming for support. You're doing it if I have to drag you there myself. Devi, give me that script."

What can I do? I hand over the paper and pray I'm not about to destroy the future health of humankind.

chapter twenty-one

Wednesday, May 28 • • • Senior Year

I see it right after I finish dinner. I see it and I squeal.

"What's wrong?" my mom asks, opening my door. "Are you okay?"

I point to the acceptance letter on my bulletin board. "I got into Tufts! That's top tier! It's ranked twenty-eighth of all the universities in the country! Twenty-eighth!"

Mom looks at the letter and then back at me. "I know, honey. We're very proud of you."

"You know?" Of course they know. I didn't just get in today.

This is all so amazing. I put Frosh on the right path and presto—Tufts, here we come! Sure, there was three and a half years of hard work in there, but I just can't remember it. I call Frosh to congratulate her as soon as Mom leaves the room. "Guess what you did," I sing.

She hesitates. "Um, I don't know."

"Come on, just guess."

"It doesn't have something to do with a certain someone auditioning for the school play, does it? Because that wasn't my idea. It was all Joelle. And then I figured, well, if it didn't come from me, then maybe it wasn't a problem. But is it?"

Huh? "What are you talking about?"

She pauses. "What are *you* talking about?"

"I'm talking about Tufts. You got in."

"Oh. Is that good?"

"Are you kidding? It rocks!"

She giggles. "Never mind, then."

"No, I don't think so. Tell me what *you* were talking about." My heart races. "What did you do? Is this about Karin? Did you tell her to do something else?"

"Um, actually, I did say something to Karin, but it wasn't a big deal at all. I swear."

She's seriously freaking me out. "What did you say?" I ask, and rub my left temple. This time-travel thing is going to age me prematurely.

"I'm trying to make her feel more confident. So she doesn't get plastic surgery. So I told her she has great boobs."

Alrighty. "And how did she react to that?"

"She thought I was being a bit weird. But I think it's a good plan! 'Cause Karin obviously has self-esteem issues, right? No matter what she does—gymnastics, cheer, whatever—she's insecure about her looks. What she really needs is her friends to make her feel better about herself."

The kid has a point. "Not a terrible plan."

"I know, right?"

I breathe out, relieved. "So Joelle told Karin to audition for the school play?"

"No, she told Tash to."

Huh? I close my eyes. Headache getting worse. "Tash wouldn't be in the play. She's not a play person. She barely speaks in public."

"That's what I thought! But she tried out!"

I shake my head. "I don't believe it!"

"I know, I couldn't either!"

This could be bad. Very bad. "Well, do you think she made it?"

"I don't know! She wasn't terrible. I mean, she was nervous, and her voice was shaky, and she's not very good at projecting, but most of the freshmen weren't that great and someone has to make the chorus, right? Do you think it's a big deal?"

Oh, God. What if she does get in? What if she's great? What if Tash's trying out changed her path for good? "What if she falls in love with being an actress and drops out of school to move to Hollywood?"

"That would suck," she says. "Unless she gets fabo roles. Like in *TTYL*. Omigod, can you check? That would be so cool."

"Not cool!" I say. "She has plans! She's supposed to go to Brown!"

"You could always go to L.A. and bring her home."

"The only way I'm going to Los Angeles is if I get into

UCLA and *that* hasn't happened yet. This is a problem." I start hyperventilating. "This is bad. Very bad. Okay, calm down," I tell myself. "I'm sure everything is fine. I better call her to check."

"Good idea," she chirps. "Call her from the house phone and leave me on the cell."

My fingers can't help trembling as I dial. The cell is pressed to my right ear, the house phone to my left. I know I look ridiculous. It rings. And rings again. Her voice mail comes on. Instead of her old message—"Hi, it's Tash. I can't come to the phone"—music blasts in my ear.

"You are the dancing queen
Young and sweet
Only seventeen!"

Houston—or, uh, Hollywood—I think we have a problem. "I'm going to call you back," I tell Frosh.

"But—"

I hang up, grab my purse, stuff my feet into my shoes, and hurry downstairs. "Mom, can I borrow the car?"

"Sure, honey," she says. I kiss her on the cheek and then run outside, slide behind the wheel, and hightail it to Tash's house.

At a red light, I let my mind wander. Tash fell in love with drama and then dropped out of school to move to Hollywood. Or Broadway. She is no longer going to Brown. She is no longer studying medicine. She will no longer find the cure for cancer.

That seems a bit extreme, doesn't it?

So she had the chorus of *Mamma Mia!* on her cell phone. She could just like musicals in this new reality. I floor the gas when the light turns green.

I pull into her driveway about five minutes later, get out of the car, lock the doors, run up the stairs, and ring the doorbell. Once, twice. Three times.

Tash's stepmom, a petite brunette, answers the door.

"Hi," I say breathlessly. "Mrs. Havens, is Tash home? I really need to speak to her."

She shakes her head. "We haven't seen Tash in a while."

Oh, God. Oh, no. She's dropped out of school. She moved to the city to be a struggling actor. All cancer-curing dreams forgotten. I knew it. "How long has she been gone?" I ask, clenching my fists. I'm going to kill Frosh.

"Since this morning," Mrs. Havens says. "She said they were ordering dinner at school. Devi, aren't you in the scenes they're practicing tonight? You're in *Mamma Mia!* too, aren't you?"

The play. The school play. *Mamma Mia!* is this year's school play. Right. I knew that. And I'm in it. "Sorry to bother you."

"Do you want to wait for her?"

"No, no, I need to get home. Just tell her I was in the neighborhood."

"Will do," she says, and closes the door behind her.

I laugh to myself. Hello, overreaction. Tash is still a student at Florence West. She just happens to be in the play. Too bad I'll have to wait until tomorrow to find out if she's still going to be premed. I reach into my purse for the car keys. No car keys? I peek through the car window and see them still in the ignition. Now what?

I'd call my mom or dad to get me, but we only have the one car. And my cell phone doesn't work.

I flip open my phone and hit send. "Frosh," I tell her, "write this down in your notebook in big letters, okay?"

"Okay," she says nervously. "Hit me."

"When you drive over to Tash's house on Wednesday, May twenty-eighth, senior year, do not—I repeat, do not—"

"Do not what?" she asks, sounding panicked. "What did I do?"

"Do not leave your keys locked inside the car."

She giggles. "Got it."

chapter twenty-two

Wednesday, September 14 • • • Freshman Year

"I think you should forget theater and do a sport in-stead," Ivy tells me later that night. "How do you feel about soccer?"

Not that I'm opposed to dropping the play, but with yearbook and trying to get As in all my classes, it sounds like I'm going to be pretty busy without taking on a new sport. But I guess I should listen to her. It's not like she's going to tell me what to do forever. Just until she gets into the school she wants. I mean, I'm guessing we'll keep talking forever. Why wouldn't we? But she's not always going to be this bossy. Right? I open my notebook to a blank page, find a pen on the living room table, and write down SOCCER. But then I imagine myself running after a ball. And tripping over the ball. Not sure if I'd be able to focus on running and kicking at the same time. "That sounds too hard."

"Don't be such a wimp," she scoffs.

I roll over on the couch. Easy for her to say. "Excuse me, but how many teams are you on?"

"That's beside the point."

"I'm not coordinated enough for soccer. I need a sport where you focus on one thing at a time. What about baseball?"

"No baseball," she says shrilly. "Absolutely not. You hate baseball."

"I do?"

"Trust me, you do. And you've never picked up a bat in your life."

"But I watched the tryout the other day and it seemed kind of fun."

"Perhaps you like watching it when cute boys play," she snaps. "But you don't like it. Next."

What has she got against baseball? Oh. She must be anti–anything Bryan. "Bowling?" I ask to test out my theory.

"Nooooo."

Yup. I have to play a sport but it can't remind her of Bryan in any way. Guess kissing is out. Not that it's a sport. Not that I would know.

"What about golf?" she asks. "You and Maya used to play mini golf, remember? You liked it. Oh, no."

"What?"

"There's only a bar left on the cell. I forgot to charge it. Where's my charger? Here it is. Problem solved. Now back to you, Little Miss Golfer."

"There's a girls' golf team?" I ask.

"No. I don't think so. Wait!" she says, her voice rising

with excitement. "You'll create a team. That will look amazing on your college applications."

I bury my face under a throw blanket. "Excuse me? How would I do that? I barely know how to play; how can I start a team?"

"You'll talk to Zetner. It'll bump up your gym mark. They already have a boys' team, so it shouldn't be that hard."

"But I'll be the only one on the team!"

"You'll find more players. You can put posters up around the school. You could even raise money for the team. Have bake sales and stuff. Mom will help. She'll love it—give you guys a chance to bond."

I hesitate. It would be kind of cool to start my own team. I'd get to design the uniforms. Hello, adorable pink golf skorts! "Fine. Except I still have no idea how to play real golf."

"You hit the ball into the hole. Easy peasy."

"I guess you're right. Dad plays, so how hard can it be?"

"Are you adopted or something? He doesn't play."

"Yes, he does. He played this summer. In that accounting tournament. He has a T-shirt from there and everything."

"You know, Frosh, you might be right. He did play. Once or twice only, but he did."

"He doesn't play anymore?" I ask.

"No more company golf tournaments after you've been laid off."

My heart plummets. "What? Dad got laid off? When?"

Silence.

"Hello?" I screech. "Ivy, why didn't you tell me?"

"Because there's nothing you can do!"

Now it all makes sense. "That's why Mom got a job?"

"Yeah."

My head pounds. "When does it happen?"

"Sophomore year," she admits.

"Poor Dad," I say.

"I know. It sucks."

"So what does he do instead?"

"He went into business for himself," she says, a bit too vaguely.

Now my head is really pounding. "Are you lying? Does he still not have a job?"

"Kind of," she admits.

"Can I call you back?" I ask. Without waiting for an answer, I hang up. I turn my phone off before it starts to ring, and run up to my parents' room.

They're both in bed. My mom is watching TV and my dad is working.

"Hey," I say, ever so casually.

"You still up?" my mom asks. My dad is sitting beside her, his laptop resting against his knees.

I nod. "Just want to see what you guys are doing."

"Relaxing," my mom says. "At least, I am."

My dad blows me a kiss without taking his eyes off the screen, and my heart breaks a little. He's working so hard, and for what? For nothing. "Dad," I begin, "how's work?"

"Busy," he says, scratching the side of his head. "As always."

"Have you ever thought about finding another job?"

"Why would I do that?" he asks.

"Because . . . because . . . yours seems really hard."

"You can't be afraid of hard work," he tells me.

"She isn't," my mom says, lowering the volume on the TV. "You should see her studying these days. She's like a different person. She's like—" She stops before she says, "Maya." "A superstar."

"What did you want to be when you were a kid?" I ask, kneeling against the mattress.

"A professional chess player," he tells me, lifting his eyes from his screen.

I giggle. "Besides that."

"A dad."

I giggle again. "Besides that."

"An orthodontist."

"Seriously? Have you seen the food that gets caught in my mouth?"

He shrugs. "I like straight teeth."

"But yours are crooked," I point out.

"I'd be my first patient."

"Well, maybe you should take some night classes." If he starts now, maybe by the time he gets laid off, he'll be able to find a new job. Or at least take off my braces.

Mom laughs. "I don't think you can just take a few classes and become an orthodontist."

"I should hope not, considering how much the kids' orthodontia costs," Dad grumbles. "Dr. Martin certainly won the job lottery."

"Except for the fact that he has to stare into people's mouths all day," Mom says.

Dad nods. "Good point. I think I'll stay where I am. What's wrong with being an accountant, anyway?"

"Nothing," I say quickly. "Nothing at all." I back out of their room and sit on the stairs. I need to think. Dad's going to lose his job. We're going to be broke, or close to broke.

We need money. Lots of money. If we had lots of money, then it wouldn't matter if Dad lost his job.

But where are we going to get lots of money?

Dad's words come to back to me.

The job lottery. The lottery. I can win the lottery. Ivy will give me the numbers and then all our problems will be solved.

chapter twenty-three

Thursday, May 29 • • • Senior Year

As soon as we pull up outside Tash's house the next morning, I know something is different, but I can't quite put my finger on it.

First, she sashays to the car. Tash, sashaying. Arms swinging, hair whipping in the wind, hips swaying. I've never seen Tash sashay. Ever.

She opens the car door with a big smile. "Hi, ladies."

Second, she's wearing contacts. And eyeliner. She looks *amazing*. Is this because of the play? It must be. How can I find out without asking, "So, have you been in school plays for the last three years? Is that why you're looking so sexy and confident?" It's weird to have your best friends changing every second. Not that it's weird for them. They don't seem to know that their lives keep changing, so I shouldn't feel guilty.

Not too guilty, anyway. And isn't it possible that this change is for the good?

If only there were a record of the last few years. Something that would keep track of plays and who was the star and whether I got my golf team off the ground—or off the green.

"Dev," Joelle says, turning in to the school parking lot, "we still have some extra yearbook cash. Do you want to order Chinese for the staff today?"

Right. There is a record. And I'm coeditor of it—the yearbook.

Joelle pulls into a free spot in the school's student parking lot, to the left of a blue Jetta. Bryan's blue Jetta. My back stiffens. Oh, no. He's still in the car. I've been avoiding this moment for four days. Deep breath. I can do this. We all get out of the car at the same time. And now he's right next to me.

"Hi," I say, swallowing hard.

He casually locks his door, like nothing is weird at all. Just another normal day at school. La, la, la. "Hey, all," he says.

Hey, all? That's all I get? *Hey, all?*

He smiles at Karin and then at me. I stare. I can't help it. I know he went out with Karin. I know he never went out with me. But doesn't a part of him remember? I search his face for recognition.

Rationally, I know that he doesn't have the same memories I do. I know he doesn't remember being with me. I know that *this* Bryan didn't go out with me.

But part of me always thought that what we had went deeper than that. That something inside him—a part of his soul, maybe, and yeah, I know that sounds cheesy—was connected to me. Was tied to me. Would remember me.

I search his eyes. They blink.

Nothing.

He has no idea who I am. Who I was. He doesn't remember me at all.

Feeling sick, I hang my schoolbag on my shoulder and slam the car door.

chapter twenty-four

Thursday, September 15 • • • Freshman Year

Before going to my first class, I visit Mrs. Kalin, the guidance counselor in charge of Interact, and I sign up. Last night, Ivy made me promise to sign up for some volunteer work, but she also assured me that involvement is pretty minimal. Meetings are Mondays at lunch.

Of course I told her about my lottery plan, but she was not so into it. Too risky. "Dad's fine," she insisted. "We don't need to win the lottery. We don't want to mess with the future *that* much." Booo.

On my way to class, I pass the school play postings. Tash and I made the chorus. Practices are Tuesdays and Thursdays after school.

I reluctantly speak to Mrs. Zetner after second-period gym.

"A girls' golf team—that's a terrific idea," she says while dribbling a basketball. "I love seeing student initiative. I might be able to find some extra money in the budget if you think there's enough interest. And I have a coaching opening Mondays and Wednesdays after school. Why don't you put up some posters and we'll meet next Tuesday at lunch?"

"Actually, I have yearbook on Tuesdays and Thursdays. Can we meet next Friday at lunch?"

On my way out, I get a text from Ivy.

```
Oh. My. God. You have no idea how superb
my arm muscles are. We are seriously hot.
Golf rules!
```

I am glad for my arm muscles. I am glad that just talking to Mrs. Zetner has made the girls' golf team a reality. But this is what my weekly schedule will look like:

Mondays: Interact at lunch, golf after school.

Tuesdays: yearbook at lunch, play after school.

Wednesdays: golf after school.

Thursdays: yearbook at lunch, play after school.

Sundays: more play rehearsal.

I'm exhausted just thinking about it. When am I going to do homework? When am I going to hang out with my friends? When am I going to sleep? Why do I have to do all the work and Ivy reaps all the rewards?

Omigod, I just used the word "reap," and not even on purpose. Why? Because last night Ivy also thought I should spend an extra hour learning SAT words. It is completely *inequitable*.

Joy is out sick today, so instead of yearbook during

lunch, I bring my food to the art room and make posters. None of my friends are interested in playing golf—Karin says it sounds boring, Joelle says she'd rather hit herself in the head with a club, and Tash says she has terrible aim—but they all help me with posters, because they are awesome. Ivy is a freak for ever losing them.

"So, I hear you have a boyfriend," Joelle says to me while sketching.

My cheeks flush. "Where did you hear that?" I ask.

"I hear everything," she says, and then laughs. "I don't get it—you couldn't just tell Bryan you were washing your hair, like a normal person?"

I sigh. "I told him I was sick but he brought me chicken soup."

"Persistent," Tash says, cutting the edges of a poster.

He gave up pretty quickly, if you ask me.

"I won't blow your cover," Joelle promises.

"Why don't you want to go out with him, anyway?" Karin asks me, arm deep in pink glitter.

"He's just not the right guy for me," I say.

"I think he's cute," Karin says. "I'd go out with him."

I almost drop my sparkles. She cannot go out with him. Ivy would freak. I would freak.

My phone vibrates before I can respond. "I just have to take this," I tell the girls.

"Oh, sure," Joelle says. "Leave us to do all the work and go take a break. Who are you talking to, anyway? Your pretend boyfriend?"

My cell vibrates again. "Maya," I lie. Speaking of Maya,

she left me a message a few days ago and I haven't had a chance to call her back yet.

"And anyway," Karin says to Joelle, "you're loving this."

Joelle nods. "That's 'cause I'm a postering genius."

She is a postering genius. Unlike us, she can actually draw. Every poster features an adorable cartoon of a high school girl in midswing.

"Good news," Ivy tells me.

I enter the hall and close the door behind me. "You got into UCLA and I can take a nap?"

"Not that I'm aware of as of yet. But Tash is still going to Brown. She's just double majoring. In premed and theater. She's balanced. She's playing the mom in *Mamma Mia!* this year, and last year she played Roxie in *Chicago*. Unlike you, who continue to be in the chorus, year after year, she's a natural."

Four years of chorus? I'm pathetic. But Tash . . . I peer through the glass window in the door and spot her slumped over her poster. Who knew?

"You have to see her, Frosh. She's so happy. And confident. Getting her to audition was the best thing you ever did."

I feel a wave of pride. "Fabo! But I can still drop out of the play, right? I mean, I'm doing golf and Interact and yearbook, so I can drop out of the play."

"I guess so. I definitely don't want to have to actually be in *Mamma Mia!* in two weeks. And come on, you started your own golf team. Who can beat that?"

I straighten my shoulders. "It really worked? The golf team?"

"Yup," she says. "You are officially team captain of the Florence Tabbies."

"Wait—we don't get a cat, do we?"

"No, of course not. Dad's allergic."

"Then why do I call the team the Tabbies?"

"I don't come up with this stuff; I'm just reading it to you. The team wins some sort of championship junior year, by the way."

Awesome! I'm a golf superstar. "How do you know all this?"

"I'm looking through the proofs in the yearbook room. And flipping through old yearbooks."

That is seriously freaky. I look at my watch. Lunch is almost over. "Hey, shouldn't you be in class?"

"Yearbook editors can take some freshman/sophomore lunches. And anyway, there are only a few more weeks of school."

The bell rings. I hear it ringing through the phone too. "I have to go."

"Later," she says.

Tash, Joelle, and Karin are putting the posters against the windowsill so they can dry.

"Thanks, guys. You're the best." I gather up our lunch remnants and toss them into the trash. Karin and Joelle are up ahead when I turn to Tash. "Listen, Tash, I've been thinking about the play, and I'm not sure I'm going to have time to do it. You know, with starting my own golf team."

She shrugs. "No biggie."

Phewf. "So you don't mind doing it on your own?"

"What? Me?" She turns pale and shakes her head. "No way. It doesn't matter. It's not like I was dying to do it. It was just a whim. I still can't believe I tried out."

Uh-oh. "No, no, no, you have to be in it."

She adjusts her glasses. "I don't want to do it by myself. It's not a big deal. I don't really care if we do it, I swear. It's so not a me thing to do."

Ahhhh! Now what? She has to do it! She loves it! She's good at it! It *is* a her thing to do; she just doesn't know it yet. But how am I going to be able to juggle all these activities plus keep up with my schoolwork? I sigh. "No, we'll do it." I sling my arm through hers. "It'll be fun."

She shrugs again. "Whatever you want, Dev. It's really not a big deal to me."

Maybe not. But one day it will be.

chapter twenty-five

Thursday, May 29 • • • Senior Year

I stay in my seat long after I hang up with her, looking at the yearbook statements. I submitted mine in March. It was basically an ode to Bryan.

Vampire Halloween, bowling, the park. It actually said *Vampr Hlwn, bwling, the prk.* You only have a few hundred characters, so you have to abbreviate.

How did I end it? *IwlLOVEu4evr.*

I flip to my page in the proofs. Instead of reflecting memories with Bryan, it says *KF,TH&JC:LUVUBFFE* and then lists all kinds of new things. Things like *Bblgumdoesnotgoinhair, Itnightmoviemrthon, 1littlebluelie, RUkidding? Myfeetrkillinme.*

I have no idea what I meant. And I never will.

I'm still feeling down when I get home. Until I see it.

Congratulations! You've been accepted to UCLA!

Holy SAT score. *She did it.* She did it!

I'd pat her on the back, but since I can't, I pat myself instead. Which is kind of the same thing. I call her right away. "You did it, Ms. Frosh. We're going to UCLA."

"No way!" she squeals.

"Way."

"I guess it's a good thing I didn't drop the play. I'm here right now, actually. At rehearsal. I can't talk long. They want us to pay attention even though we're not doing anything. It's kind of annoying."

"Well, whatever you did, it worked. The acceptance is smack in the center of my bulletin board, looking gorgeous. UCLA, here I come. Wait a sec." Uh-oh.

"What? Did it change?"

"No, it's still there." I rummage through the other papers on my board. I find a pile of college stuff and go through it too. "It's just that there isn't anything about a scholarship."

"But we didn't get a scholarship to Tufts either, did we?"

"No. We didn't. But . . . we need one. How else are we going to afford it with Dad out of work? I guess we can get a loan. But then I'll have to spend the rest of my life paying it back."

"Lot-te-ry! Lot-te-ry! Lot-te-ry!"

"Frosh, no. You're just going to have to work harder."

"Are you kidding me?" she screams. "I can't work any harder. It's physically impossible!"

She so belongs in the play. Such a drama queen. "No need to get hysterical," I say. "We can talk about this later. I'm sure there's a way to get a scholarship. Maybe if you study a bit more, or join another team—"

She groans. "Why don't you do something for a change? Like give me the lottery numbers! I'm tired!"

"My job is to help you!"

"Okay, if you don't want to do the lottery, let's just invest in something. You can tell me what the good stocks are. Then we don't have to worry about paying for college at all. Yeah. We can just buy a college and then go there."

I roll my eyes. "I don't think UCLA is for sale."

"But we can still buy stocks! You can tell me what's going to be hot, and presto, college tuition. And—"

She's drowned out by a very off-key group of students singing: *"Ever as before, ever just as sure . . ."*

"Can you go somewhere quieter? I can't hear you."

"Yes, I could go home. How about that?"

I sit down on the corner of my bed. "Can't you just sneak into the hallway?"

"Tale as old as time—"

She sighs. "One sec. I'm on the move. Okay. Where was I? Right, stock buying."

"Sounds a little bit like insider trading," I tell her. "I don't think it's legal, never mind ethical."

"It's wrong to give someone else tips. But not to give yourself tips, right?"

"I'm not sure."

"We should do it! We can make a million! Then we don't even have to go to college."

She is *so* immature. "Of course we have to go to college. It's not just about getting a job afterward; it's about learning. And the experience." I'm reminded of my grad statement and how little of it I understand. When I get to UCLA, I'm going to make sure to remember everything. "Maybe we could consider buying shares in a company. A company that's going to be worth a gazillion dollars by the time you're my age. Except—"

"What? I love the plan. Don't ruin the plan. I can help. I'm an economics genius, you know."

I roll my eyes. "What are we investing exactly? We have no money."

"Oh. Right. That is a problem."

"Maybe you should join the Junior Traders Club," I tell her.

"No," she says desperately. "No more clubs. Can't I ask Mom or Dad? Do they know anything about stocks?"

I wish. "If they knew anything about stocks, we wouldn't be in this situation now, would we?"

"We need to be more creative. Maybe I should invent something before it comes out! Like the Internet!"

I giggle. "Wouldn't you feel bad stealing someone's invention?"

"I guess so," she admits. "Then back to my original suggestion . . . the lottery! Think about it. It's a victimless crime. You get to go to college. It won't matter that Dad gets laid off. Mom won't have to work either—unless she wants to."

"But what about the risks? What about Karin's upcoming boob job?"

"What about Tash's future awesomeness?"

She does have a point. "They must keep records of the winning numbers, no? Hold on." I hop over to the computer and start searching. "One sec . . . Yes, they do. They post all the winning numbers for the last ten years." I pause. "Should we really do this?"

"Yes!"

I scroll down for more info. "They seem to have one every three days. And there's one tonight. Your tonight. And the jackpot is"—holy moolah—"twelve million." I could be a millionaire. By tonight. Although, technically, if she becomes a millionaire tonight, I'll have been one three and a half years ago. Show me the money! Then again . . . "Shouldn't we feel bad for the people who were supposed to win tonight?" I continue scrolling. "Wait. No one else was going to win! Next time, the jackpot just goes up to fourteen million."

"So the next winners will just win two million instead of twelve?"

"Exactly."

"Not too shabby," she says. "I told you—it's a victimless crime."

"Okay," I say before I change my mind. "Let's do it."

"Yay!" she chirps. "What will we buy first?" she asks, her voice filling with awe.

"A car," I say. "Definitely a car. My own car. And an extra one for Mom and Dad so they don't have to share."

"I could use some new clothes. Designer clothes! Ridiculously expensive ones!"

Ooh, there was a gorgeous coat I saw in *Seventeen* last month. And Bella has some new superb tops in for summer. But Frosh better not blow all my car money—I mean my tuition money—on a new wardrobe. Although with twelve million, we can certainly blow a teeny-weeny bit of it. We should also use the money to do some good stuff. We'll sponsor Tash to find the cure for cancer. We'll help other students pay for college too. Hey, if this works, I can get back to my Change the World list and start . . . changing the world!

"So what do I do?" she asks.

Does she need me to spell out everything? "I give you the numbers and you walk into a store and buy a ticket."

"Don't you have to be eighteen?"

Oh, yeah. "You better bring Mom."

"You think Mom is going to buy me a lottery ticket? Are you crazy? She never buys those things. She says they're like throwing away money."

"You'll have to convince her, then, won't you? Call her and ask her to pick you up from rehearsal. Tell her you need to get some school supplies. Then, when you're at the mall, get her to buy the ticket. Easy peasy."

"I'll try," she says. "I'll have to think up a good reason."

I can think up twelve million.

chapter twenty-six

Thursday, September 15 • • • Freshman Year

"So," Mom says after we've loaded up the cart with extra school supplies, "you're really taking class seriously these days."

"Yup," I say.

"You've been so busy all week," she says.

"It's all the activities," I explain.

"Are you sure you're not taking on too much?" she asks, expertly navigating our cart around the pharmacy. "You need to have time for yourself. And your friends. And boys," she says, and wiggles her eyebrows.

"There are no boys," I say. Unfortunately.

"But what about the nice boy who came by over the weekend?"

Nice? If she knew what he was going to do senior year, she might not be calling him nice. "He's just a friend."

"You don't have feelings for him?"

"No," I say quickly.

"Well, there you go. You have to trust your feelings. Too bad, though. He was cute."

Tell me about it. Can't dwell on him, though. He's not meant to be. On the other hand, what is meant to be is my future new wardrobe. "Hey, Mom," I say extra nonchalantly, "can we also buy a lottery ticket?"

She laughs. "What? Why?"

"Because it's twelve million dollars?"

"Yes, but your chance of winning is about one in twelve million."

"Someone has to win." I wave my hands in the air. "Why shouldn't it be us?"

She shakes her head. "Why don't you just take the dollar and toss it in the wishing well? It's just as much of a waste."

That's what she thinks. "Please, Mom? I had a dream last night that we won. I think it's a sign. Just once. I have a really good feeling about it. And you just told me I have to trust my feelings. Please? I'll even pay for it myself."

The corners of her mouth twitch. "With the allowance we give you?"

"Exactly."

She pushes the cart toward the cashier. "All right, dear. One lottery ticket. This *one* time."

After all this, we'd better win. Which we will. Ivy checked the numbers. Although, as I've seen, time travel can sometimes mess things up. Or what if she read me another day by mistake? Or what if I wrote the numbers down wrong? I glance at my palm, where I transcribed said numbers. I didn't want to pull out the notebook in front of my mom. And I was afraid that if I wrote it on a piece of paper, it would get lost among all my other papers. I hope the numbers didn't smudge.

We approach the counter together.

"All this and one lottery ticket," Mom says. "My treat."

So sweet, my mom.

"Which one?" the clerk asks.

"NY6," I say.

"Your numbers?"

I covertly read them off my hand: "Five, forty-four, sixteen, nine, eighty-four, and twenty-six."

Mom raises an eyebrow. "Where did you come up with those?"

"Oh, um. Well, five is the number of . . ." Of what? "Pens I have in my pencil case. Forty-four are the last two digits of Tash's number. Nine is a lucky number. Everyone knows that. Sixteen is Dad's birthday." Wahoo! One that doesn't sound like a lie! "Eighty-four is what I got on my, um, French quiz . . . and twenty-six is how old I'm going to be when I get married!"

She laughs and squeezes my arm. "You got an eighty-four on a French quiz? I'm impressed."

If she's impressed with an eighty-four, wait till she sees my UCLA acceptance. She's going to pass out with awe.

The cashier prints out the ticket and hands it to me.

"Do you want to see a movie?" Mom asks after we pack up the Volvo with our new purchases.

I'm about to tell her that I have a lot of homework when I see her eager smile. "What do you want to see?" I ask.

"I have no idea," she says. "I haven't seen a movie in ages. I don't even know what's playing."

I can't help feeling bad. I mean, with my dad working all the time, my mom never gets to go out. And anyway, once they announce the winning ticket tonight, it's not like I'll be able to concentrate on schoolwork. I may not even go to school tomorrow. I think you're allowed to take off the day to celebrate after you win twelve million bucks.

"Sure," I say. "I haven't seen a movie in a while either." I was supposed to see one last Saturday with Bryan but that wasn't allowed to happen. "I hear *101 Possibilities* is really good. Let's see that."

We should do a normal mother-daughter activity before everything changes, anyway. Of course, she has no idea life as we know it is about to change.

We're going to be rich!

Really rich. Not just a teeny-weeny rich. Multimillionaire rich.

Normally when life as you know it is about to change, you're not even aware of it. You ask Karin, the girl sitting next to you in class, if you can borrow her highlighter, and you become best friends. Or your best friend cuts your bangs and then you hate the mirror for the rest of the third grade. Or you go to a party at Celia King's house, spill salsa on a couch, and develop a full-blown new crush.

Let's forget about that last one.

Normally you don't know when your life is about to change. But now I know. And it's so exciting. Life is exciting. I swing my purse, lottery ticket inside, and try to hide my smile.

chapter twenty-seven

Thursday, May 29 • • • Senior Year

Whoosh! You know how people say life can change in an instant? Yeah, well, my life just changed in an instant.

I mean everything.

One minute I was hurrying down the carpeted stairs to get a glass of water, and the next I was slipping down a marble staircase.

I grab the banister and straighten myself out.

My house is different. Or maybe I'm in a different house? My house does not have floor-to-ceiling windows. My house does not have four floors. Where am I? I carefully hike back up the steps. I appear to be in some sort of mansion.

A mansion! The lottery ticket must have worked. She must have bought it. Yes!

I run down the stairs and up the stairs and then back down. This place is the size of a train station. Did we buy a train station?

"Careful, Miss Devi," a voice from the sky says. "I just washed ze floors. You don't want to slip and break your neck."

Just kidding—not from the sky—the voice comes from a small plump woman wearing a black dress and a white apron. My housekeeper? My housekeeper!

"Hello," I say, freezing in my spot. I definitely don't want to break my neck. Although if I did, I could just tell Frosh not to run on the stairs and then everything would be A-OK. I really am a superhero. A superhero with a housekeeper. How superb is that? I wonder if I have a cook too. Or a driver. Or a butler. I giggle to myself as I run back up the stairs. Carefully. Even if I *can* call Frosh and tell her not to slip down the stairs, I bet it would still really hurt.

The floor-to-ceiling window to my left shows a big circular driveway. With three cars. Clarification: three Mercedes.

One of those *must* be mine. Wahoo!

On the top floor, I discover six closed doors. Which is my room?

I open one—a closet. A huge stacked closet, filled with all kinds of intricate-looking soaps and shampoos and fluffy towels.

Next—my room. Definitely my room! The most perfect room ever. My books are on the shelf, so I know it's mine. My bed. Oh. My. God. My bed! It is a dream bed! A high canopy bed piled with pastel throw pillows. Forget superhero—it's a princess's bed. I can't help myself; I dive right into it. The comforter is satiny smooth. I sleep on a giant marshmallow. Yay!

I really might stay in bed forever.

Except I have to explore the rest of my mansion.

I slide off my bed—I'll be back, sweet marshmallow, take care!—and head toward my closet. My huge, ginormous closet. My—I pull open the door—walk-in closet. I glide inside and can't believe my eyes. There are rows and rows of clothes. A row of high-end jeans, a row of glimmering tops (all hung up! How fancy am I!), a row of silky dresses. Where do I wear these, exactly? Afternoon tea, anyone?

Does my mansion have afternoon tea? I think it might.

Oh. My. God. My prom dress!

It's in a delicate clear plastic cover that says *Izzy Simpson* across the side, but it's my dress. It looks just like the silver drapey one I had before but darker and slinkier. And probably twenty times the cost.

I must wear it immediately.

I toss off a pair of designer jeans and a buttery T-shirt, neither of which I remember putting on. Oh, look—I'm even wearing different underwear. Lacy. With a French label. Who knew rich people wear different underwear?

I slip on the dress and admire my reflection in the floor-to-ceiling backlit mirror that's right beside a pretty vanity table topped with antique brushes and combs and professional-looking makeup and velvety jewelry boxes.

Am I the queen of England? I think I might be.

I look around my room to see what other treasures I have. Lots. A flat-screen TV. A paper-thin laptop. A really lush carpet.

A mural.

Yes, instead of the plain lavender color that used to be on my walls, my room is now painted to look like a garden. With trees and flowers and a lake.

I still have the pictures on my table. I grab them to see who they're of—no Bryan. Phewf. They're mostly of me and my friends, although there's also one of me and my dad on some kind of boat. I go on expensive vacations? Excellent!

I peek through the blinds and out the window. Wow. This isn't a backyard. This is a view of the entire city. I think I'm on Mount Woodrove. And—a tennis court! I have a tennis court! Do I play tennis? I guess I do. Maybe Frosh should join the tennis team too. I bet I have cute tennis outfits. I bet I have a whole room of tennis outfits— because I have the biggest house in town!

Is there a house this big in town?

I don't remember seeing a house like this. Even from the outside. We must have had it built. And the view looks kind of familiar. . . .

Wait a sec. It's the Morgan Lookout! On Mount Woodrove! Where Bryan and I tried smoking! And looking out over the lookout is a pool. An infinity pool.

Wowza.

There is someone in my infinity pool—a dark-haired, buff, tanned man in a tight black bathing suit. Why is there a dark-haired, buff, tanned man in a tight bathing suit in my pool? I drop my blinds and hurry down the stairs, careful not to slip. Now, how do I get outside?

I scurry into the kitchen (huge, glossy, high-tech, with a marble island in the middle and all kinds of gleaming silver appliances) and wave to the housekeeper (who's now wearing plastic gloves and scrubbing the sink).

Meow!

Huh? I look for the noise and spot a tiny cat with a leopard-like coat stretching her arms in the corner. Hah—I guess the house is so big that the cat doesn't affect my dad's allergies. Or maybe my dad and the cat have separate wings! I head through a back door that leads outside to a huge planted terrace.

I'm going to have the best parties. I bet I've already had the best parties!

I feel an unexpected twinge of weirdness—kind of sad that I don't remember the superb parties I've already had—but keep moving. I almost run over my not-bigger-than-a-size-2-silver-bikini-clad mom. She's wearing a matching sarong, huge white sunglasses, and jeweled flip-flops.

Oh. My. God. My mom's gone glam!

"Where's the fire?" she asks.

"Hi!" I say, giggling. "Taking a swim? Enjoying the pool?"

"Yup! I'm just taking another dip and then Alfonzo and I are going to heat up the barbecue. Have some pink lemonade."

"Don't mind if I do," I say. We have a chef named Alfonzo! How crazy is that? I pour myself a glass as she removes her wrap, drapes it over one of the deck chairs, flutters down the steps, and submerges herself in the deep end of the pool. The pool where the dark-haired buff man in the tiny bathing suit is now lying on an inflated orange raft. Could that be Alfonzo, our chef? Our super-hot chef.

Mom glides through the water, toward the man, and plants a kiss on his lips.

"Mom!" I scream. "What are you doing?"

"Kissing my husband?" she says with a laugh, then splashes him.

The glass of lemonade slips out of my hands and shatters against the deck.

"Honey, are you okay?" She takes a look at my surely horrified expression. "What's wrong? Are you getting sick? I hear there's a bug going around."

Kissing her . . . husband? I feel light-headed, like I'm on a high-speed elevator shooting to the hundredth floor.

Her husband? The hot guy is her husband? Alfonzo is her husband? What happened to her other husband? *My dad?*

I think I might pass out. I need to get back inside immediately. I retreat into the house, out of breath and panicked. I need to figure out what's going on. I hurry through the kitchen and into another room. Where can I find family pictures? What happened to my dad?

I need my dad.

I run through the house, looking for clues. Where are their wedding pictures? What about the shot of the two of them at their anniversary dinner that used to be over the living room mantel? What about our family shot at Disney? Do we even have a living room mantel?

Where's my dad? What if something . . . happened to him?

I run back up to my room—don't slip, don't slip—and open all the remaining bedroom doors, looking for him. "Dad?" I whisper. "Are you here?"

I find what must be my mom's room—king-sized bed, dressing room . . . but there are no signs of my dad. Where are his brown bathrobe and Mickey Mouse slippers?

I hurry back to my room and rummage through my stuff for an explanation. Tacked to the wall are hundreds of postcards. Who from?

Dad?

I unpin one of the Eiffel Tower.

On the back it says *Love you, honey! Can't wait to see you this summer on the Riviera!*

My dad is in France? I'm going to the Riviera? Or maybe I've been to the Riviera? I turn to the picture of me and my dad behind my princess bed. Was that picture taken on the Riviera?

Can't. Breathe. Why is my dad in Paris while my mom is in the pool with her new husband?

It makes no sense! My parents love each other! Sure, they've had their problems over the years, but they still love each other. Don't they? I sink to my super-lush carpet.

The lottery. It ruined my parents' marriage.

Where is my phone? I need to call Frosh right now and tell her to cancel. Last time I used it, it was right over . . . there. I think. The polished desk has no phone on it. So where is it?

I run back downstairs. "Excuse me," I say to the house-keeper. "Have you seen my phone?"

"On ze glass table in ze den," she says.

Superb. Now, where's the den? I sprint from room to room until I find a glass table.

On this glass table is an iPhone. Huh. Normally I would be excited to find out that I am the proud owner of an iPhone. Except if that's mine, then I would have gotten rid of my old cell.

I feel faint and grab on to the edge of the table to steady myself. If I got rid of my old phone . . . if I replaced it with the iPhone . . .

. . . I will never speak to Frosh again.

And next time I see my dad, I'll have to be speaking French. I hold up the iPhone with trembling hands.

What. Do. I. Do?

The photo on the screen of the phone is of a sexy Italian man. Alfonzo. Which means . . .

Unless I have a highly inappropriate crush on my step-father, this is probably my mom's phone. Or Alfonzo's. You never know. He could like himself a lot.

It's *not* mine.

I search the rest of the house—the rest of the ginormous house. Where is my phone?

Eeeeeeep!

That was my phone! I know my phone! That's the sound it makes when it's running low on battery! When it's down to one bar, it beeps every hour or so. I know that sound. Must find that sound! Where did it just beep from?

Upstairs. It must be in my room. I run back upstairs—don't slip, don't slip—and start rifling through my drawers. Why do I keep so much junk? Everything I've ever written, read, or bought is in here. Everything but my phone.

My bed. It must be in my glorious bed.

I dive back inside the marshmallow and find it buried underneath one of the hundred pillows, princess-and-the-pea-style. Yes! My phone, my three-and-a-half-year-old decrepit phone is right here. Safe and sound. That was close. I cradle it in my hands. I'm so smart. Even though I could have bought a new glamour phone, I must have kept this one because I knew how useful it would one day be. I glance at the battery. Only one bar. I wonder why that is. I definitely charged it last night. Didn't I? Let me worry about one problem at a time. First I have to call Frosh and get her to fix this mess.

Instead of ringing, it says, "Hiya, this is Devi. I'm out and about and can't take your call—"

Ack. Why isn't she answering? There's no time for this. There's no time for voice mail! It's already almost seven. The drawing is at ten.

I redial. Voice mail, again. Where could she be?

chapter twenty-eight

Thursday, September 15 • • • Freshman Year

I'm getting kind of excited. I'm going to be rich! In five minutes, when they air the numbers, I'm going to be very, very rich. How rich? Money-spilling-out-of-my-Prada-purse rich.

Any minute now.

What will I buy first? Izzy Simpson clothes!

I knock on my parents' bedroom door. "Turn on your TV. They're going to announce the numbers."

My mom and dad are already in bed, Dad in his bathrobe and Mom in her pink pj's. Dad got home early tonight—nine-thirty. Maybe once we win, he can relax a bit. It's nice to see them in bed together—although I wish they were cuddling. They could definitely use some couple time. Maybe now they can take a romantic vacation together. For more than a long weekend.

"What numbers?" Dad asks.

"The lottery numbers."

"Your daughter claims we're going to win," Mom says.

Dad laughs. "If she does, can I quit work and stay home with you?"

"If we win, I'm opening a bakery. Banks's Bakery. *You* are welcome to stay home."

"Sounds good to me. I'll stay home and play chess."

"I want to stay home too," I say, falling back onto their bed.

"So where's this lucky ticket?" Dad asks.

Whoops. "In my purse. One sec!" I run back to my room and look for my bag. I hear my mom turn on the TV and get the station ready. I rifle around for the ticket. Imagine I lost it? No, here it is! Here we go! My fingers also graze my cell. Another whoops. I forgot to turn it back on after the movie. I click the power button and see that I have messages.

Fifteen messages.

Uh-oh.

First message: "Where are you?"

Second: "Answer the phone!"

Third: "Don't buy the ticket!"

Um . . .

Fourth: "You probably already bought the ticket, right? That's why everything changed. We have a real problem!"

What does this mean? What should I do? I need her to call me this second! What if she's trying to call right now? And she can't, 'cause I'm listening to the messages?

"Come on, hon!" Mom calls.

I walk toward their room. Slowly.

One step. Two.

I pause outside their door. Now what?

"They're starting right after the commercial," Mom says. "Get the ticket ready!"

Ring, cell phone, ring! What am I supposed to do? I step inside.

"We're back in thirty seconds with the winning lottery ticket numbers," the announcer says.

Uh-oh.

"Devi, what numbers are we rooting for?" Dad asks.

"Five," I say nervously. "And then—"

My phone rings.

Oh, thank goodness.

"One sec, I have to take this," I say, clicking it on. "Hello?"

"You answered! Finally! Where were you? Never mind, never mind, there's no time! You didn't win yet, did you?"

My eyes flick from the TV to my parents sitting comfy in the bed to the ticket flapping in my hand. "In like ten seconds."

"Rip it up!"

"What?" I must have misheard.

"Rip it up! You don't want to win! Trust me."

"Are you kidding? I can't do that. Not now."

"You have to," she orders.

"It would, um, look really weird." I can't make a whole production out of the lottery and then rip up the ticket.

"And we're back," says the announcer. She has shiny bobbed hair and a perfect smile. I bet she had braces. "For

tonight's NY6 drawing on Thursday, September fifteenth."
Inside the glass box she's standing behind are six numbered
balls spinning above air hoses.

"I heard that!" Ivy screams. "You can't win! Make it
stop!"

The first ball pops out of the vacuum and perches on a
ledge. The announcer gives us all a big toothy smile. "And
the first number up is five."

My parents whoop.

"What do we have next?" Dad asks.

"Um . . . we have . . ." Oh, shoot. What do I say?

The second ball pops. "The next number up is sixteen."

Mom looks at me expectedly. "Don't we have that? For
Dad's birthday?"

"Um . . ." Ahh! "Not sixteen."

"Seventeen!" Ivy screams into my ear. "Say you have
seventeen!"

"Seventeen," I repeat, shaking my head.

"I could have sworn you told me sixteen," my mom says.
"So close."

"The third number up is . . . forty-four," the announcer
says.

"Tell them we have forty-five," Ivy orders.

"That just sounds dumb," I say into the phone. "Forty . . .
three," I say instead.

"Oh, sure, that sounds much better," Ivy mutters.

"Are you going to explain why we're doing this?" I
whisper.

"Yes. Later. But right now, just don't win. No winning.

No Alfonzo. And destroy the ticket as soon as you get a chance. Got it?"

"But what about my new clothes? What about tuition? And who's Alfonzo?"

"Just do it!"

Eeeeeeeep!

"What was that?" I ask.

"It beeps every hour," she says.

"Do you need to charge it?"

"Frosh, can you focus on the task at hand, please?"

I go through the rest of the numbers, calling out slightly different ones.

"So that's it?" Mom says with a loud exaggerated sigh. "Told you, Devi, you might as well have thrown the dollar away."

"But then we wouldn't have had this lovely bonding time," I say with a tight laugh. I stuff the ticket into my pocket.

Back in my room, I study the lottery ticket in my hand. I think of all the amazing stuff I was going to buy. Clothes! Cars! Fancy trips! Am I really going to rip it up? Seems like a crazy thing to do.

Although Ivy did make it sound important . . . and I guess we can always buy a new lottery ticket next week. I hesistate before sadly ripping the ticket into a million pieces and letting them flutter into my garbage pail like confetti. Very sad confetti.

I don't know who this Alfonzo character is, but he owes me a new Izzy Simpson wardrobe.

chapter twenty-nine

Thursday, May 29 • • • Senior Year

Ouch! I'm climbing down my marble staircase, minding my own business, when—poof—hello, carpet burn. A girl could break her neck like this. Once again, I'm on my old carpeted stairs. All the changes have reversed themselves. I'm back in my boring old house. With my boring old view. Boring old Dad? Holding my breath, I hurry to my parents' room and knock. "Hello?"

"Come in, honey," Mom calls. ·

I push the door open. Mom's reading a novel; Dad's sitting, wearing his bathrobe, his back propped up by pillows. His slippers are happily waiting for him at the foot of the bed. I can't help smiling. "Hi," I say. I dive face-first onto the bed and throw my arms around both of them in a hug.

When I finally get back to my room, I plug my phone into the charger and climb onto my perfectly soft, perfectly lovely, boring old bed.

chapter thirty

Saturday, September 17 • • • Freshman Year

On Friday night, I saw *101 Possibilities* with the girls. I still had fun, even though I knew the ending.

Today I'm supposed to spend the day doing my chemistry homework, and reading economics, and practicing my French conjugations, and studying for my upcoming algebra test and my upcoming American history test, and starting my paper on *Jane Eyre*, but then Karin calls me and invites me to go to the mall, so I go. She lends me her American history tapes, which she's already listened to. Now all I have to do is listen to them.

But I need the weekend off.

Of course I don't tell Ivy that. She is all freaked out, because the phone doesn't seem to be charging. "I don't get it," she says later that evening. "I've plugged it in for two nights straight. Why isn't it working?"

"What do you think will happen if it dies?" I ask her while getting dressed for Kellerman's house party. "Will your life keep changing every time I do something different?"

"It didn't change before we started speaking," she said. "So I'm thinking it'll stay static if we stop. I'm guessing my life only changes when you do something differently because of our conversations, you know? Anyway, it's not going to die. I'm going to figure out how to fix it. But for now let's use it sparingly."

Mom drops me off at Karin's first, and we do our whole getting-ready ritual: makeup, the dabbing of perfume, head check for dandruff, and breath test. This time I add a new one.

"I wish my boobs looked like yours," I tell Karin, checking myself out in the mirror.

"I don't know why you keep saying that," she says, blushing.

"They're the best shape! Trust me. Girls around the world would kill for your cleavage."

"Hmmm," she says, taking a peek at herself in the reflection.

Joelle's mom picks us all up, and off to the party we go. We're looking adorable, if I do say so myself, boobs and all.

"Jerome Cohen's here," Karin whispers to Joelle. "You have to talk to him."

"Definitely," she says, her eyes twinkling.

"He's really cute," I tell her, but I'm thinking, If Jerome's here, does that mean Bryan's here? Not that I care. Okay, I care a little. "We should go talk to him!"

We maneuver our way over to the couch, where Jerome is hanging out with two other guys. Sadly, there's no Bryan in sight.

"Hey," they say.

"Hey," we say.

La, la, la.

What do I have to do around here to get a conversation started? Drop more salsa on the couch?

"Having a good weekend?" I ask them.

"Not bad," Jerome says, drumming his fingers against a side table and giving me a cute smile. Not exactly "dimples"-worthy, but still cute. "You?"

"Great," I say. La, la, la.

"Do you girls know Nick and JT?" Jerome asks.

We all say hello and introduce ourselves. Nick mumbles hello but doesn't look up. He's obviously shy. I can kind of see why too: his skin is really bad. His nose and chin are covered in rashlike pimples. Poor guy. His over-gelled hair and flannel button-down aren't helping matters either. He's shuffling his sneaker-clad feet.

"So, Nick, what middle school did you go to?" I ask him.

"Carter," he mutters.

"Oh. Cool," I say. I wait for him to ask me something in return. He doesn't.

So I turn to JT. Unlike his noncommunicative friend, he has perfect skin. He's definitely cute in a leather jacket, gelled-hair sort of way. He could easily play Danny if the drama department ever decides to put on *Grease*. He's also a bit sunburnt, although the spot on his face where he was wearing his sunglasses is pale.

"You got some serious color," I tell him.

He smiles. "I know, huh? It's the worst. I have a ridiculous farmer's tan too." He rolls back his sleeves so I can see his forearms. His tanned *and* well-muscled forearms.

"I'm guessing you weren't farming," I say. Not too many farms in the area.

"Golfing," he says with a lazy smile.

"Really?" I lean toward him. "You play?"

He nods. "I have a handicap of fourteen."

I have no idea if that's good or not. I haven't done my golf homework yet. "You know," I say, "I'm starting a girls' team at Florence West."

"No way." He inches closer toward me. "You're a golfer?"

"Not yet," I admit. "But I'm gonna learn."

He looks me up and down. "I'm going to hit some golf balls tomorrow. Wanna come? I can show you some moves." His eyes linger a little too long for his so-called moves to be purely sports related.

I think he's asking me out. "That sounds fun," I say. But then I wonder. Should I go out with him? I'd better ask Ivy. He's cute. Isn't he? I don't know what to do. Is this what it's going to be like for the rest of my life? Never trusting myself to go out with a boy because I have to ask . . . myself?

"Actually, I may have plans for tomorrow. But I'm not sure. Can I get back to you?"

"No sweat," he says, stretching his arms above his

head. "Lemme know. I'm going to get a drink. Want something?"

"I'm good, thanks." I give him my best hidden-braces smile. Now I just have to wait for her to call.

Ten minutes go by.

Twenty minutes.

Thirty.

A watched phone never rings, does it? But *why* hasn't she called yet? It's almost nine-thirty! Doesn't she want to see how I'm doing? I'm used to her calling me every hour or so to check in.

What if something happened to her? How would I know? What if the phone does die? I send her a text that says Ivy! Call me! Urgent!

Ten more minutes. Twenty. Thirty.

My phone finally rings. "Thank God!" I squeal.

"Thank God what?" a voice asks. Not Ivy's. Shoot.

"Who is it?" I ask, annoyed.

"It's your sister. Hello? I've been gone less than a month, and you've already forgotten about me?"

I feel a pang in my stomach. "Oh, hi, Maya! Sorry. Hi! How are you?"

"I'm good. I miss you! We haven't spoken all week!"

"I've been really busy," I say. "You know."

"Of course. Me too. I was wondering if you still want to come visit for Columbus Day weekend. Should we ask Mom and Dad to get you a ticket?"

"Oh, um, yeah. Sure. That sounds like—"

Beep!

Yes! Call-waiting. Caller ID says it's me. "Maya, I gotta go. Can I call you back later?"

"Sure. Don't forget about me. We'll need to get you a ticket soon, because prices—"

Beep!

"I really have to go, Maya. I'll call you tomorrow!" I hang up and switch over to Ivy. "It's about time!"

"What's wrong?" she asks. "It better be important. We're low on battery."

"I know, I know. I just need to ask you something." I duck into a corner. "A guy named JT asked me out."

"Who?"

"JT," I whisper. "I don't know his last name. He's cute. He plays golf! He wants to hit some balls with me tomorrow. Can I go?"

"JT Prause?" she asks.

"I don't know."

"Does he have dark hair? Does he look like he could play Danny in *Grease*?"

I love how we think alike. "Yes!"

"Then no," she says. "You absolutely can't go out with him."

My shoulders slump. "Why?"

"Because he's a tool."

"Really?" I ask doubtfully. "He seems nice."

"He's not. He's a loser. A *big*-time loser."

"That's not a very nice thing to say," I huff. "And anyway, if he's friends with Jerome Cohen, he can't be that big of a loser."

"I don't mean he's not popular. He's a loser *in life*. He doesn't even go to school anymore. He has a major gambling addiction. He stole from half the class and racked up like thirty thousand dollars on his parents' credit card and they sent him to Heken. You know—the school for delinquents."

"Oh." Never mind, then. I do not want to go out with a guy who goes to Heken. I don't even want to associate with a guy who goes to Heken.

"Plus, last year he sold Jenny McIntosh's bra on eBay."

"He did not!"

"Uh-huh," she says. "Do not go out with him. He's a sketchball."

"He *seemed* nice." Although he was checking me out in a slightly skeevy way.

"He isn't. Do you want him to sell *your* bra on eBay?"

"I wasn't going to give him my bra. I was just going to hit some golf balls with him."

"Don't. He'll take your credit card while you're not looking."

"I don't have a credit card. You do?"

"You get one next year. If you're good. If you don't go out with thieves. Why don't you read up on golf instead? Yeah, that's a good place to start. Spend the day reading about golf techniques. Did you finish all your homework today?"

"Uh-huh," I lie.

Eeeeeeeep!

"Damn, that's the battery again! I have to figure out how

to fix it. I'm going to a party at Laura Kingsley's. I'll be home late, so I may not call."

" 'Kay. Bye!"

"Bye!"

I hang up and drop my cell back into my purse. While I'm in there, I make sure my wallet still is too.

chapter thirty-one

Saturday, May 31 • • • Senior Year

Right before Karin picks me up, I stare at my still-uncharged phone. What's its problem? I had it plugged in all last night, and it looked like it was charging. The red light was on and everything. But I still have less than a bar of battery. I really need to go to MediaZone tomorrow and get them to fix it or give me a new battery or something.

When I hear the honk, I toss the phone into my purse and run outside. We go through our regular ritual.

"Hair?" she asks, leaning over.

"Dandruff-free." I lean over and tilt my head.

"You too. Breath?" She blows into my face.

"Minty. Me?"

"Scopey."

"Perfect."

Next we pick up Joelle, who's dressed in an emerald

tunic over jeans, and then Tash, who looks—well, there's no other word for it—stunning.

She's wearing her usual—jeans and a black shirt—but these are skinny jeans and she's accessorized them with black stilettos and a pale yellow scarf around her neck. Her hair is blow-dried and glam, and the contacts and the little bit of black liner make her eyes pop. Wowza.

As soon as I walk into the party, I spot Celia sitting on Bryan's lap. The chicken fingers I had for dinner almost make a reappearance. "I need a glass of water," I tell the girls. "Come with me to the kitchen?" We all go.

Sitting on the kitchen counter beside the party's host, Laura, is my possible make-out partner, Harry. Is he back to being my prom date?

"Hi, Harry," I say with a nervous giggle. "Nice to see you. Do you know where I can find a Coke?"

I expect Harry to say hello. To possibly give me a come-hither stare. But he doesn't even notice me. Did I scare him off? Or did I scare Frosh off? Did my hookups with Harry disappear faster than Alfonzo?

"Hey, babe," I overhear Harry say to Laura. "What color should your corsage be?"

I reach inside the fridge and pull out a bottle of Coke. Laura's chin has telltale red marks. So I guess that's why I'm not going to prom with Harry. I scared Frosh off and now Laura is the one kissing him and being his prom date. Keeping track of my love life is giving me a headache. I turn to my friends. "I think I need some fresh air."

"Me too," Joelle says.

"Me three," Karin says.

A crowd of seniors is already outside, including another potential minefield: Sean Puttin, the preppy jerk who said I kissed like a fish.

Unless Frosh did her job and remembered to keep her fish lips to herself. But how will I know? Asking—hey, everyone, did I make out with Sean Puttin?—is probably not the best way to find out.

"Hey, do you know where Sean is going next year?" I take a sip of Coke and try to sound nonchalant.

Karin's eyes flash. "To hell?"

Hmmm. It seems like I still kissed Sean Puttin. Thanks for nothing, Frosh.

"I'm still so pissed at him for saying I kiss like a fish last year," Karin says angrily.

Huh? Now Karin kissed him? Karin wouldn't have kissed him if I had. Unless I never did, and Karin kissed him instead!

Karin fingers a curl. "Whatever. I know my lips are too thin. Although Stevey seems to like them as is. And anyway, at least they'll be perfect by college after the lip injections."

I choke on my Coke. "You don't need lip injections! You don't need a boob job either. You look great the way you are!"

Her eyes widen. "Boob job? Why would I get a boob job? Do you think I need a boob job?"

"No!" I shake my head vehemently. "Absolutely not!"

She wiggles her upper half. "I have nice boobs. But I definitely need to fix my lips."

I deliberate using up more of my potentially precious minutes and decide that, yes, I have to help Karin. When I have the chance, I secretly text Frosh: `Good job with the lavish boob praise. Keep Sean Puttin away from Karin too. V. imp!`

All this juggling past and present is kind of exhausting.

After dropping the cell back into my purse, I find my friends deep in a discussion about corsages. It's prom fever. I check the area for Tom Kradowski. Is he here too? I should probably get to know him.

"Have you seen Tom?" I ask Karin.

"Doesn't he go to his dad's on the weekends?"

I should probably know that. "Right. Of course." I can't believe I'm going to prom with someone I've never spoken to. Assuming he's still my prom date. "Am I going to prom with him?"

Joelle laughs. "Yeah. Speaking of prom, there's Jerome."

Tash rolls her eyes. "Enough with Jerome. Can't you forget about him already?"

Joelle crosses her arms defiantly. "What's your problem?"

"It's just *enough*. He broke up with you *three* years ago. It's time to move on. It's time to stop obsessing over him, stop going to his shows, and stop waiting for him to ask you to prom. He's not going to."

Ouch. Tash is being harsh. On the other hand . . . it has been three years. Hasn't it? I can't keep track anymore.

"Can't you just go with someone else?" I ask, trying to make peace.

"There isn't anyone *else* I like," Joelle snaps. "Letting him slip away was the biggest mistake of my life. I wish you guys could understand that. I'm going inside. Later." She spins and walks away without looking at any of us.

Tash sighs and grabs a handful of pretzels from a plastic bowl. "She's such a drama queen. I don't even think she likes Jerome. She just likes the idea of being a tortured artist." She waves at someone across the room.

I look in the direction she's staring in and see Nick Dennings with his arm around Elle Mangerls, his sophomore girlfriend. He's wearing a button-down shirt and jeans, but he definitely has a geeky-cute thing going on. He laughs at something his girlfriend says, and it's a nice belly laugh, one that echoes around the room.

"I heard his parents bought him a plane for graduation," Karin whispers.

"Are you kidding me?" I ask. That seems insane. "Like with a crew and everything?"

"No—a small one. That he could fly."

"How does he know how to fly a plane?"

"He's been taking lessons," Tash says.

Imagine—having your own plane. Or having a boyfriend who has his own plane. Maybe I should go out with him. Not now, obviously—he has a girlfriend—but as a freshman. And he's supersmart. And has a great laugh. So what if he had acne? He grows out of it. He's a superb long-term investment. It would be nice to have a boyfriend again. And Nick would have to be a better boyfriend than Bryan. At least he wouldn't one day decide he wants to move to Canada.

I excuse myself to call Frosh. "Hey," I say.

"What's up?" she asks. "I thought you were trying to save battery."

"I am. But I have an idea. Since you're so desperate to have a boyfriend—"

"I am not!"

"Whatever. Do you know Nick Dennings?"

"Um, yeah."

"Go out with him," I say.

"*Nooooo.*"

"What's wrong? Don't judge him by his acne." She's so superficial.

"It's not *because* of his acne. I tried talking to him tonight, and he was completely lame."

"Give him another chance. He's a *great* guy."

"Why, what does he do?" she asks with interest. "Cure cancer or something?"

"Not everyone can be on the cancer-curing track," I say. "He's smart. And has a great laugh. And he has a plane."

"Excuse me?"

Eeeeeep!

Even though the sound gives me a mini heart attack, I ignore it and rush on. "He's getting his own airplane! How cool is that? His mom sold her Internet company for a ton. Plus, his acne clears up and he's actually really cute. You should lock him up early. He's a keeper. He'd probably pay for our college too. And think of it—I could fly anywhere I want this summer! L.A., Miami, wherever!"

She laughs. "You want me to go out with someone *now* because in three years his *mother* is going to be rich?"

"It sounds kind of crass when you say it like *that*."

She sighs. "If I went out with him now, wouldn't I have to stay with him until senior year?"

"I suppose."

"That's a lot of time for a trip to South Beach."

"It's not *just* for a trip to South Beach." Although that would be fun.

"I'm not dating some guy with the personality of a wet sponge just so you can get a free trip. Sorry."

"Just talk to him again! That's all I'm asking. Give him a chance. Please?"

She clucks her tongue. "I'll talk to him again. But that's it. If there are no sparks, I'm giving up."

"Deal." Oh! I have a brilliant idea. "If you don't like him . . . see if Joelle does!"

"But she's still obsessing over Jerome Cohen," she says cluelessly.

"Exactly! Let's get rid of Jerome Cohen. That relationship was obviously no good for her. If she falls for someone else instead, she won't be obsessed with Jerome."

"Ha. You just want to have a best friend who has a boyfriend with a plane."

I laugh. "It can't hurt."

chapter thirty-two

Saturday, September 17 • • • Freshman Year

I find Karin, Joelle, and Tash on Kellerman's living room couch. When I spot Nick Dennings standing by himself, fiddling with an iPod, I wave him over. I definitely don't think he's the right guy for me, but I'm happy to play matchmaker and try to fix him up with Joelle.

He looks at me, looks away, and then looks back at me. He seems unsure if I'm actually motioning to him.

I wave again.

He blushes in a "who-me?" way and then shuffles over.

"What are you doing?" Karin whispers.

"Isn't he kind of cute?" I say. "He's smart too. I think he's a way better catch than Jerome Cohen."

"You're crazy," Joelle says under her breath.

"Hello," Nick says. "I'm Nick."

Er. "Yeah, we met before," Joelle says, rolling her eyes. No, I don't think the two of them are going to hit it off.

They're kind of like water and oil. Or water and a cell phone. And not in the good way.

"Sorry," he says, blushing.

"I never remember people either," I hurry to say. "I have the worst memory. It's a problem."

Nick cocks his head to the side and smiles. "If you're not part of the solution, you're part of the precipitate."

Huh? Was that English?

Tash laughs. A big, deep, hearty laugh.

"I don't get it," Karin says.

I shrug.

Joelle's gaze bounces between Nick and Tash.

"Old science joke," Tash says, blushing.

Interesting. Very interesting.

chapter thirty-three

Sunday, June 1 • • • Senior Year

There's a loud knock on my door on Sunday morning.

Early Sunday morning. Seven-thirty on Sunday morning.

"Hon?" my dad says, opening the door. He's dressed in pleated khaki pants and a crisp white shirt. "You're still in bed? We tee off in half an hour. You better get a move on."

Huh? Obviously something has changed but I don't understand what. Why is my dad up so early? Why is he not in his bathrobe? Why is he looking fit? "We're going for tea?"

He laughs. "We're playing golf. In half an hour. Get moving. I just put on a pot of coffee."

Seriously? I jump out of bed. I don't think I've seen my dad out of bed this early since before he lost his job. And we're going to play . . . just the two of us? What if we have nothing to talk about? And how does one play golf exactly? And what does one wear to play golf? I open my closet door and rummage through my stuff. Can I wear jeans? I have no idea.

I happily discover a pleated white skort, a pale pink shirt, and a matching cardigan that I've never seen before. These must be for golf. Good. One problem solved.

I put them on, find a pair of sport socks in my drawer, tie my hair back into a low ponytail, and hurry downstairs for a cup of coffee.

I pull my arms and shoulders back and swing. Not only does the ball connect with my club, but it goes soaring over the lush green public course.

I am a golf natural. It's so weird. I don't consciously know what I'm doing, but my body does. As soon as I felt the club in my hand, I knew what to do. Apparently I have a handicap of ten. I have no idea what that means.

"Great shot!" my dad says, giving me a thumbs-up.

So far, we're having a great day. A wonderful day. The sun is shining. My dad and I are bonding. We haven't had such a nice time together since . . . well, I don't remember the last time.

The tip of my nose feels hot and I reach into my bag and dab on some extra sunscreen. "Dad, come here. The back of your neck is burning."

He strolls over and turns around. "What would I do without you, kid? I'm really going to miss you when you're at UCLA."

He knows about L.A.? Of course he knows about UCLA. If it's on my wall, then it's in my life. "I'm going to miss you too." I'm just getting to know him again and now I'm moving to the other side of the country!

"And I don't want you to worry so much about the tuition. I'm sorry the golf and academic scholarships didn't come through, but it's the right time to sell anyway."

Huh? I close the lotion and put it back into my bag. "To sell what?"

"The house," he says, and then pulls his clubs along.

My jaw drops and I chase after him. "You're selling the house?"

"Not again," he says. "We've been through this. Your mother and I just don't need four bedrooms anymore. Your sister rarely comes home, and with you on the other side of the country—I'm sure the two-bedroom condo in town will be just fine for us. Cozy."

Uh-oh.

chapter thirty-four

Monday, September 19 ● ● ● Freshman Year

When I slide into my seat for the first period of the day, Madame Ritale purses her lipstick-smeared lips (she tends to get it on her teeth) and says in French, "I hope you all did your homework, because we are having a pop quiz!"

Um . . . I never got around to doing my homework this weekend. I needed to decompose. I mean decompress. I mean . . . I forget. I did not review my SAT words this weekend either. I did spend four hours on Sunday at play practice and another four hours researching golf. Yup, Ivy got to play golf with Dad while I had to research it. When I heard the news, the jealousy felt like a lit match in my chest.

I stare at the test paper. I blink. I look up. I look back down.

If no one was watching, I'd take out my phone and text my future self: `Aidez-moi!`

Or maybe: Au secours!
If I knew which one, I wouldn't need help, would I?

"Please pass your homework assignment up to the front," Mr. Durst, my chemistry teacher, tells us. I probably should have done that, huh?

Ms. Lux scans the entire room.
Don't pick me, don't pick me, don't pick me.
She stops on me. "Devi, can you please describe for us three ways to deal with scarcity on a national level?"
Ivy is going to kill me.

I accidentally-on-purpose leave my cell phone in my locker for the rest of the day so I won't have to hear Ivy screaming at me or read any nasty text messages. When the final bell rings, I brace myself before opening my locker.
"Wanna go to the mall?" Karin asks me.
"Oh, um . . . maybe. Let me just check if my mom called. . . . She needed me to . . . um . . ." I take out the phone. "Clean my . . . teeth today."
Karin laughs. "What? Clean your teeth? What are you talking about?"

No new messages! No new texts! Yes! I unclench my shoulders and turn to Karin. "Oh, I meant my braces. I thought I might have an orthodontist appointment, but I don't. Never mind. I'm good. I'm all for the mall."

No new messages means nothing has changed. Yet.

And maybe nothing will change. It was only a few assignments. One little day of mistakes. How much damage could I have done in one day?

chapter thirty-five

Monday, June 2 • • • Senior Year

Congratulations on your acceptance to Hofstra! I read.

Huh? Hofstra? What the heck? I was two acceptance letters up from Hofstra! Yesterday we were going to UCLA! My parents were selling the house so I could go to UCLA, so it wasn't an ideal situation, but still. They were not selling the house so I could go to Hofstra.

I pick up the phone to call her, and I see there's only half a bar left. My palms feel sweaty. Why isn't it charging? I need to go to a MediaZone store. I was planning on going yesterday, but by the time I got home from golf, it was closed.

I hear some static. "Ivy? Now's not a great time," she says. "Can you call me in a few hours?"

Excuse me? My body stiffens. "How can now not be a good time? We're running out of battery. Now *is* the time. Now might be the *only* time. And you need to explain to me why I lost my UCLA acceptance. And what could you possibly be doing that's more important than talking to me?"

"Going to the mall," she admits.

"The mall? You're going to the *mall?*" I draw out the word like it's a disease. How could she be shopping at a time like this? She should be sitting around waiting for me to tell her how to fix the big fat mess she's made. "Can you try to be responsible, please? We have a slight disaster on our hands. There's time for the mall later. Where are you exactly?"

"At the bus stop," she says. "Karin, Tash, Joelle, and I are waiting for the bus, and—oh, wait, here it is—"

"You're not going," I order. Why does she have to be so selfish?

"It's only for an hour. We're gonna look at jeans and get a Cinnabon. Can't we do our stuff later?"

"I have other things to do later! And what if the phone dies later? Huh? What then?" I know I sound like a big whiner, but I can't help it. I need her to tell me what happened.

"Okay, okay," she says.

I hear Karin ask, "Dev, you coming?" in the background.

"My mom needs me at home," Frosh lies. "You guys go ahead. I'll see you tomorrow."

"Everything okay?" Karin asks.

"Everything's fine," Frosh says, sounding miserable.

"Now, can you please tell me what happened?" I ask.

"Why?" she asks nervously.

"We're going to Hofstra again! What happened? Did you drop out of the play? Or golf? Or yearbook?"

"No! I'm still doing all three," she says, her voice cracking. "Plus Interact!"

"Well, you did something," I huff. "The admissions letter on my wall is not lying."

She sighs. "It started with a pop quiz."

"In what?"

"French."

I throw my free hand up in the air. "So? You speak French."

"Barely! And I didn't have a chance to do my homework this weekend."

Is she trying to kill me? We have a plan! "Why not?"

"Because I was burnt out! And I needed to relax! Last week was really busy and I needed some time for myself! And the cell phone might be magical, but it doesn't make me more time! I can't do everything! I relaxed on Saturday but I spent all day Sunday at play practice and researching golf!"

"Well, you have to learn how to balance your time properly. It's one of the lessons of life. I've learned to balance mine, haven't I? It used to be all about Bryan, and now it's—"

"All about bossing me around?"

"*Nooooo*. It's all about school. And friends." And making sure she doesn't screw up. I close my eyes and rub them so I don't have to look at the sad letter on my wall. "This is really bad, Frosh. Do you *want* Mom and Dad to sell the house?"

"No," she squeaks.

"Then you have to work even harder to get a scholarship now that the whole lottery thing isn't going to come through. Do you think you failed the French test?"

"Yes," she says, her voice as deflated as a week-old helium balloon. "I'm pretty sure I did. And I also handed in some algebra homework that may have had a few mistakes in it. And Ms. Lux called on me in economics and I didn't know the answer."

Eeeeeeeep! I close my eyes.

"Haven't you charged it yet?" Frosh asks.

"It's not working, okay?"

"Why not?"

"I don't know! I'm trying to fix it!"

"So you think this could be it? The phone could die and then we'd never speak again?" Is it my imagination or does her voice sound hopeful?

"Not if I can help it," I say. "But if our talking time is going to run out for good, you have to listen to me while you can."

"Okay, you're right," she says with a sigh. "So what should I do?"

I take a deep breath. "For one, you have to be careful with Ritale. She loves those pop quizzes. I think she gave one a week. She also loves getting lipstick on her teeth. Have you noticed?"

"Yeah. And thanks for the quiz warning," she grumbles. "That would have been terrific info *yesterday*."

I *should* have thought of that earlier. I probably have that quiz somewhere too. "Wait a sec. I bet I kept it." I drop to my knees and rummage through the drawer under my bed.

There are papers. Many papers. At the bottom of the stack are the ones from ninth grade. I rummage through the ones that are in French. Quizzes. Two per week, on Mondays and Fridays. "I kept them all," I say. "The quizzes from June. May. April. March. February. January. December. November. October. September. September nineteenth."

"That's today!"

I fall back on my behind. "It certainly is." The red F stares me in the face. "And you certainly failed."

"How do you know?" she asks.

"Hello? I see it. A big fat F, with a note that says *Devorah, la prochaine fois, faite ton devoir!* Which means 'Next time do your homework.'"

"Blah."

I flip through all the other quizzes and read out the marks. "C, D, C, D . . . Ahhh! What's wrong with you? I didn't get crap marks like this!" Sure, I had Bryan to help me, but still. These marks are *bad*.

"I don't know why," she whines. "I'm just not good at French. And anyway, you have me doing too many things! I can't keep up!"

"We need to fix this."

"How?"

A fluorescent lightbulb pops on in my head. I look at all the papers. Ninth grade. Tenth grade. Eleventh grade. Twelfth. All here. All in my hands. "Oh. My. God. I have everything. All the tests. All the papers." But can I do it? It's definitely morally wrong. But what are my choices? If I don't, I may never get to go to UCLA. And my parents might have to sell the house. "Frosh, do you know what this means?"

"We need to be better recyclers?"

"Or . . ." My voice drifts off.

Silence. "You're kidding," Frosh says. "Right? We can't look at your old papers and tests." She giggles nervously. "You're the one who was so worried about cheating."

"I know it's risky. I know the lottery fiasco scared us. But this is different. This is all my work. I'm just cheating off myself. It's not *really* cheating. I did all the work, so you don't have to. And who knows how much time we have left? Normally my phone dies less than a day after the beeping starts. I know this phone is . . . special, but it could die at any second. It's our responsibility to take advantage while we can."

"I don't know," she says.

"You said you were burnt out. Now you don't have to be. What would you rather be doing tonight? Watching TV or studying for . . ." I flip to the freshman section and rifle through the tests. "American history. You have a test tomorrow, you know."

"I know!"

"So which is it?"

She hesitates. "Watching TV."

"Exactly. We were wondering how to fit everything in. Now we figured it out." I figured it out. See, Bryan? I don't need you. I can make it on my own. "Take out your notebook and get ready. Your entire life's about to change."

"Let's hope not," I hear her mumble.

chapter thirty-six

Tuesday, September 20 • • • Freshman Year

"Devi, can you hold on a second?" Ms. Fungas, my American history teacher, asks me as I'm sprinting to get some lunch before yearbook.

My heart starts hammering immediately. I mean, why would Fungas want to talk to me? A teacher should not want to talk to me a few hours after I cheated on a test. This is a very bad sign. I've had a frog in my throat ever since I copied all the questions and answers for today's and tomorrow's tests and assignments last night, but would Ivy listen to me? No.

Instead, she dictated my essay on *Jane Eyre*. I had to type fast, because she didn't want to waste the battery. She tried plugging the phone in while she used it, but it still didn't charge.

"Yes?" I ask, timidly approaching her. My heart races.

What if the answers to the test changed somehow over time? Or what if Fungas knows? But how could she know? Maybe she hasn't even marked them yet. Or maybe I failed. Maybe—

"I took a look at your test paper," she begins, looking at me over her moon-shaped eyeglasses, "and—"

I bombed. I must have. Ivy's going to kill me.

"—you got an A. By far the highest mark in the class. And I was wondering—"

If I cheated? My heart might explode.

"—if you would be interested in being a peer tutor."

Huh? "Sorry?"

"I have been asked to recommend top students to help other struggling students. Would you be willing? You'll only have to see two students a week and you'll get extra credit. What do you think?"

"Oh, um . . ."

Tutor in history? I would never have passed the test if Ivy hadn't fed me the questions. Plus I have no time. When am I supposed to do this? My after-school hours are pretty much all booked up.

But I can't just say no to something without discussing it with Ivy. She'd kill me.

"Why would you want me to be a tutor after only one test?" I ask.

"It wasn't an easy test," she says, smiling. "And I have a good feeling about you."

You wouldn't if you knew my study practices.

"If you're interested, just pop by the peer tutoring room and tell the guidance counselor. Take the night to think about it. And congratulations. Well done."

It doesn't feel well done. I hurry to my locker to get my lunch money. Then I hurry to the cafeteria; grab a turkey sandwich, an apple juice, and a bag of salt-and-vinegar chips; and dash to yearbook.

And skid to a halt before I smash right into Bryan.

"Good stop," he says with a smile. "We nearly had another collision."

I can't help smiling back. "I'm learning."

"Where are you off to?"

"Yearbook meeting," I say, slightly out of breath.

"Good for you," he says. "I guess that means you don't want to come outside with me and enjoy the gorgeous day? I have my very own bench that I'd be happy to introduce you to."

"You do, do you?"

"I do. I'd be willing to share it, though."

"Thanks," I say. "But I can't." For many, many reasons.

"You sure? It might be one of the last nice days," he says. "What about after school? Want to get an ice cream?"

"Bryan, I—"

He smiles again. "A purely platonic ice cream."

I laugh. "I would, but I have play practice."

"You *are* busy. What are you doing tomorrow? Soccer?"

Golf practice won't start until next week. Think fast, think fast. "I'm peer tutoring. American history."

"All right, but if you change your mind, my bench would love to meet you. It even likes salsa." He waves and heads to the cafeteria. Yeah, I know Ivy hasn't given me the okay for tutoring yet, but I don't need a future-telling device to predict that she'd rather I tutor than have ice cream with Bryan. Even though I really like . . . ice cream.

chapter thirty-seven

Tuesday, June 3 • • • Senior Year

On my way to lunch, I spot Tom heading out the front door. He's very tall. I'm definitely going to stop by the mall and get some higher heels. I wave. He hesitates before waving back.

Hmmm. I buy a plate of mac and cheese and then I almost drop my cafeteria tray when I see Nick Dennings sitting at our lunch table. How did that happen?

Go, Frosh! He's sitting right between Joelle and Tash, so Frosh must have made it happen at the party and forgotten to tell me. Forget prom limo! I might be taking a prom plane!

"So," I say, smiling at Joelle, "who's getting picked up first on Friday?"

"Karin and Stevey at Karin's then Tash and Nick—at Nick's—then me, then you, then the prom."

Au revoir, Tom. I guess I'm going stag. Probably less painful than making conversation with a guy I don't even know. Maybe I'll buy myself a pair of awesome flats. Wait. Tash and Nick? I look back and forth between the two of them. Who knew? How did I miss that before? They're the perfect couple!

"I guess I have to accept that Jerome just isn't going to ask me, huh?" Joelle says, leaning her chin against her palm. "Maybe I should have said yes to Kellerman."

"Too late now," Tash says. "He's bringing Elle Mangerls— you know. The sophomore."

This is getting confusing. It's like musical dates. And poor Joelle. It's one thing to go stag because that's what she wants to do, but it's another to go stag just because she was waiting for Jerome Cohen to ask her. I need to remind Frosh to help her get over him already.

"We're going to have the best time," Karin gushes. "Best prom ever! And I finally bought an iPod for the flight."

What flight? "Wait a sec," I say. "Are we taking Nick's plane to the prom?"

Everyone stares at me. "Since when does Nick have a plane?" Tash asks.

"Doesn't Nick have a—" Oh. Never mind. "Forget it. What plane, then?"

"The flight to the Caribbean?" Karin says. "Where Nick's new island is?"

Tash rolls her eyes. "I can't believe your mom bought you an island for graduation. Who does that?"

"I can't believe she's flying us all there for prom week-end," Karin says. "She's the best."

Wowza. New shopping list: flats, new phone battery—
it's still not charging!—and one rockin' bikini.

I jam my key into the door and run up the stairs. I know
it's going to be better. I know it's going to be better. She has
the answers; it has to be better. I know, I know, I know, I
know. Is it UCLA? Did I get my acceptance back? Please,
please, please, let me have gotten my acceptance back.

Congratulations! You've been accepted to Harvard.

Harvard.

Harvard!

Harvard Harvard Harvard.

Oh. My. God.

Forget UCLA. I topped UCLA. I beat Maya. I got into
Harvard! The number one school in the country! This is
insane.

I search around to see if there's any scholarship info, but
I don't find anything.

Okay, so I haven't made it yet. I mean, Harvard is amazing, but obviously I need to get a scholarship. I can't let my
parents sell the house to send me there. I just can't.

I call Frosh.

"We got into Harvard," I tell her breathlessly, and then
burst into a fit of giggles.

"Are you kidding me?"

"Nope."

"That's insane!"

"I know! Even Maya only got into UCLA! We are officially smarter than Maya!"

"Oh, wait. Speaking of Maya, she wants me to come visit. On the Columbus Day weekend."

"What are you talking about?" Why is she rambling about Columbus Day when I'm trying to discuss Harvard?

"Maya? Our sister? Wants to see me?"

"Yeah, I know who she is, thanks. I just don't know what you're talking about. You're not going to visit Maya. You never visit Maya."

"Are you telling me that in four years, I never—not once—go visit Maya at school?"

That doesn't make me sound very nice. "You're too busy!" I huff.

"How can I be too busy for my sister?"

"Whatever. You are."

"What exactly did you do for Columbus Day, freshman year?"

I think it might have involved a couch, a bunch of movies, some blankets, and my then boyfriend. But she doesn't need to know that.

"You were with Bryan, right?" she presses.

"Perhaps," I admit.

"Well, I don't have to do that. I don't care how busy I am. I'm going to see Maya."

"We'll see." She can't just jet off for the weekend. What if I need her to do stuff here? Who knows what could happen in California? She could upset the whole time-travel continuum. And what if crossing the time zones will screw stuff up? Until I'm at Harvard with a full scholarship, I'm not taking any chances. No, until I'm married with two kids, I'm not taking any chances. No, until I'm—well, I'm never taking any chances. As long as the phone works, she'll have to listen to me. No matter how exhausting it is—for either of us.

"I'm going," she says.

"You're not if I say you're not," I snap.

"Hello, control freak."

I am not a control freak. I am not. At least, I never used to be. Maybe she's made me into a control freak. "What if you go and something bad happens?" I retort. "What then, huh?"

"What could possibly happen?" she asks. "I get a tan?"

"Your plane could crash." I know it's a mean thing to say, but whatever. It could happen. Although I probably shouldn't be talking about crashing planes when I'm about to take one to the Caribbean. Maybe I shouldn't bring that up to Frosh just yet. Anyway. "Remember the lottery? We didn't think that winning twelve million dollars would lead to Alfonzo."

She sucks in her breath. "Omigod, you're so selfish! You don't care if I crash! You only think about yourself!"

"Are you even listening? You *are* me. And anyway, it could happen," I say, softening my voice. "Anything could happen. That's why you have to stay the course. Anything different you do can have major repercussions."

"Why is me going to visit Maya dangerous, but me using your tests and papers not?"

"Be-because I wrote those tests and papers!" I stutter. "It's not the same thing. At least, I don't think it is." My head starts to pound. I can barely tell what's right and what's wrong anymore.

"Maybe I should stop using your old tests, then?" she asks hopefully. "Just in case."

"No way," I say. "We are not sliding back from Harvard to Hofstra. I need to give you the answers to everything. For the entire four years."

"Are you kidding me?"

"No! Plus you need to step it up a little."

"Step it up? Why?"

"Because we may have gotten into Harvard, but we can't afford it. We need a scholarship. Where are you now?"

"Play rehearsal. I'm always at play rehearsal."

"Okay, good. I have to go to the mall."

"Why do you get to go to the mall and I'm stuck at play practice? I hate play pratice! I don't even have any lines!"

"Because *I* need to figure out how to fix our battery situation. And MediaZone is in the mall." And I need new shoes for prom and a bikini for post-prom, but I should probably just keep those bits to myself. No need to rub it in. "If you get home before I do, catch up on your reading."

"Why? I thought I don't have to anymore now that I have all the tests."

"You should still keep up with your reading," I tell her. "What if a teacher calls on you in class? Do you not remember what happened in economics on Monday? Do you want to go to Stupid State? Or do you want to go to Harvard?"

She pauses. "Honestly, I don't really care."

"Trust me. You will."

"Well . . . I was asked to be a peer tutor. Do you think that will help?"

"Absolutely!" I tell her. Devi Banks, peer tutor! Who would have thought?

"But how am I supposed to help people do their history homework when I have the worst memory in the world?" she asks. "Maybe I shouldn't do it."

"Don't be stupid," I snap. Yikes. That was mean. Have I always been this mean? Ever since the Bryan breakup, I've gotten so . . . hard. She brings it out in me, though. She's giving me a serious headache. Can't she see how close we are to getting everything I—we—want? I'm not going to feel guilty about this. I'm doing this for *us*.

"I just might not be able to help it," Frosh says. "Nature versus nurture and all that."

"Frosh, I take it back. You are not stupid. *We* are not stupid. And this is a fantastic opportunity." We're so close I can taste it. "It'll get us a scholarship to Harvard for sure."

"Get *you* a scholarship to Harvard, you mean."

"Get *us*. Us. It's all about us."

"Is it? I just want to go to the mall."

"Try to think a little bit more long-term, will ya?"

"I *do* want to go to a good college. But do I really need to go to the *best* college?" She sighs. "How am I supposed to tutor when I don't understand anything?"

"I'll help you." *Eeeeeep!* Or not. The battery warning comes on every half hour now. Scary.

🔌

I call Maya as I'm walking through the mall. I want to make sure she knows I got into Harvard. Can't criticize me when I'm at the number one school, can she?

"Hello there, brainiac," she says as soon as she picks up.

I guess she knows. "Hi," I say smugly. "How are you?"

"Great! Packing. I can't believe I'm off to Europe in two weeks!"

"I'm sure you'll have a terrific time," I tell her.

"Sure you don't want to come with me? I don't know why you have to take summer courses to get ahead. Wouldn't you rather take some time off?"

First of all, summer courses? Seriously? And second, she's still criticizing me? I got into the top school and now she's telling me I work too hard? "I don't need time off," I snap.

"You sure? You sound like you do. We'd have so much fun! Lots of pizza in Italy you could eat upside down."

"I can't. I have too much to do."

"A little fun wouldn't kill you," she says. "A European boyfriend maybe . . . You've worked your butt off for four years and you deserve a break! A little romance! Balance in your life is healthy."

I'm starting to regret having called her in the first place. This is why I stopped wanting to talk to her when she went away to school. Back then she kept telling me that I spent too much time with Bryan. I didn't want to hear it, so I stopped calling her back. I stopped telling her everything. I told Bryan my secrets instead. He took me under his wing. Why did I always need to be under someone's wing?

I shake my head. I can't believe now she's telling me I spend too much time working. She should make up her mind already.

"I have to go," I tell her when I reach MediaZone.

"Devi—"

"I'll speak to you next week, okay? Bye." I hang up before she can say anything else. A European boyfriend! I can't believe Maya is telling me I need to find a boyfriend! When have I ever had a problem dating guys?

Although I am going stag to prom.

Whatever. I walk over to the clerk at the front desk, put my phone on the counter, and explain my charging problem.

He nods for a while, then opens a new lithium battery and puts it in. "Hmmm. This doesn't seem to work," he says. "That's odd."

"Tell me about it."

He picks up the phone and studies it from different angles. "I'll be right back." Five minutes later, he returns with a rectangular box. "Here you go," he says with a big grin.

"You fixed it?" I ask hopefully.

"Even better," he says. "Since you've had the phone for over two years, you're eligible for a new one."

I throw the box back across the counter. "I don't want a new phone! I want my old one."

He blinks repeatedly and hands me back the box. "But this one has Bluetooth. And a navigator."

"I don't care." I shove the box back over to him. "I need *my* phone."

"But it doesn't work."

"So make it work!"

"I can't." He shrugs. "Sorry."

He returns my original, Bluetoothless, navigationless, battery-deficient phone. There's only a half bar left. Now what?

chapter thirty-eight

Wednesday, September 21 • • • Freshman Year

I stop by the peer tutoring office before leaving school.

"Ms. Fungas sent me," I tell the guidance counselor. I feel ridiculous saying her name out loud. "I'm supposed to sign up to tutor American history."

She waves me in. "Outstanding! You can start right now. A student popped by at lunch asking for help. I told him to check back after class in case we could accommodate him."

What? "Today?" I wasn't expecting to have to start *now*. Sure, I paid extra attention when Fungas reviewed and explained the answers today, but it's not like I know them by heart.

She gives me a thumbs-up. "Isn't that great?"

The back of my neck starts to tingle. "But, um, I don't even know what I'm doing."

"I'm sure you'll be fine, dear, or Ms. Fungas wouldn't

have sent you. It's just another freshman. He's in Ms. Fungas's other class and wants to review his last quiz."

"Oh, I don't think I can do it. I'm so sorry, but—"

"Here he is," the guidance counselor says.

I turn around.

Bryan.

He smiles at me. My entire body flushes.

"So, Devi, what do you think?" the counselor asks. "Are you up for it?"

"Yes," I say without missing a beat. "I'm up for it." Maybe Ivy doesn't have to know.

"Hello?"

"Oh. My. God!" she screams.

"Omigod what?" I ask, glancing at Bryan. Oh, no. She's going to kill me. I push back my chair. "He was just—"

"We did it! We're going to Harvard with a full scholarship!"

"We what?"

"It worked! The peer tutoring! Full scholarship! To Harvard!"

"Really?" I squeak.

"Yes! That peer tutoring totally worked! Wahoo!"

"Awesome! But I have to go. I'm here right now. Tutoring." I hesitate. "Nothing else has changed, right?"

"No. Why would it have? The letters from Harvard are here. Pictures of my friends are here. Nothing's changed.

Besides the scholarship. Wait, who were you talking about before? 'He' who?"

"No one," I say quickly. "The head of peer tutoring. He wasn't sure if I'd be good at this."

"Obviously you are. 'Cause we are in! And—"

Ivy continues rambling about Harvard this, Harvard that, but instead of listening, I'm staring at Bryan.

Sweet Bryan. Funny Bryan. Dimpled Bryan. "I really have to go," I tell her again.

"Right," she says. "Have fun. Sorry for interrupting. I'll call you later."

I hang up and turn the phone off. "Sorry about that," I tell him.

Bryan is sitting across from me in one of the tutoring rooms, looking as adorable as always. I know I should have told Ivy who I was helping, but if it doesn't change anything in the future, then it doesn't really matter, right? If I had somehow gotten us back together, she would have noticed. Yeah. She definitely would have. The pictures would be all about Bryan again.

It's not like we're making out or anything. Not yet. Ha. Kidding. I've been helping him with the quiz. He forgot his, so I've been using mine as a springboard to explain the concepts. It's kind of fun, actually. Who knew? I can teach! You don't really have to remember all the details when you're explaining it. It's mostly about understanding what happened and why. Cause and effect, something I'm an expert on these days.

Cause: I didn't say no to tutoring Bryan, and now he's

only a foot away from me. Smelling very yummy, like buttery popcorn.

Effect: every time I inhale, it feels like kernels are popping throughout my entire body, from my stomach to my toes. In a good way.

"So, how is Ivan?" he asks.

The name startles me, but then I remember that I told him that was my boyfriend's name. "He's good."

"So what else have you been up to?" he asks. "Besides continuing to have a boyfriend."

"Oh, you know." I shrug. "This and that."

"You seem really busy all the time. Stressed."

"I am," I admit.

"So spill," he says, reaching across the table and putting his hand on my elbow. "What's weighing you down?"

Pop, pop, pop! His hand is on my arm! He's touching me! Must remain calm. It's not like it matters. It doesn't matter. I can't like him. I'm not allowed. He's no good for me. I pull back so his fingers fall to the table. "I'm under a lot of pressure," I say.

"What pressure?" He clasps his hands together above the table.

I wish he were still touching me. "Well, for one, the pressure to get into a good college."

He tilts his head to the side. "College? You're worried about college already? In the first month of high school?"

I bite my lip. "When you say it like that, it does seem kind of early."

"Are you planning your college courses too? What about

your job after college? Are you putting money into your re-
tirement fund?"

I laugh. "What, you don't worry about the future?"

He shrugs. "I worry about the present. I try to enjoy, you
know? The day. The sun. My bench."

I giggle. "You love that bench of yours, huh?"

"Why, yes, I do. I'd be happy to share it with you, if
you'd like to check it out."

"Why, thank you."

"You're welcome. It encourages relaxation."

"I could use some relaxation," I say. "I'm just so nervous
about messing anything up."

"You just need to chill," he says. "And maybe more sleep?"

I twist a lock of my hair. "Am I looking tired?"

He flushes. "I didn't mean that you don't look good. You
look great. You always do."

Pop, pop, pop!

"You just seem overburdened," he adds.

I am overburdened! "It's all the extracurriculars. I'm taking on too many."

He shrugs. "So drop some. Which do you hate?"

"All of them. No, that's not true. I like organizing the
memories and photos in yearbook. But being in *Beauty and
the Beast* kind of sucks. It takes a lot of time and I don't even
have any lines."

He laughs. "I think you'll make a very cute tree."

"Thanks. But I'm actually a chair in the Beast's mansion. Mostly I just sit there and . . . well, act like furniture."

"I'm sure you'll make a cute chair. Though I hope no

one sits on you. But I'm also sure they could find a replacement chair if they needed to."

"I know, but if I drop the play, then Tash will drop it, and it's really good for her, so I can't. Plus, I signed up for Interact, which I can't drop, because who drops their volunteer work? That would just make me a bad person. Oh, and there's golf."

He raises an eyebrow. "You play golf?"

"No. But I'm starting a girls' team."

"Why do you want to start a team when you don't even play?"

"My dad plays. Kind of . . ." I stop talking before it gets too confusing. "So you see, there's nothing I can drop. Besides, all the activities will help my college applications." I press my lips together. Enough about me and my boring college obsessions.

When did I get so boring? When did I forget to enjoy the bench? And those who sit on it.

"What about you? Are you doing any activities? I saw you trying out for baseball."

"You did, did you?"

I blush.

"Then you saw my spectacularly awful performance. I didn't make it. But I've been playing with some friends in town, so it's no big deal. Oh, and I've been thinking of taking up the drums. I kind of suck at the moment, but I'm having fun."

"Good for you. You're very well rounded. Colleges will love you." Great, there I go again.

"I haven't given college quite as much thought as you have," he says with a smile. "Although my dad would love it if I went to school in Montreal. That's where he lives."

"Does Montreal have good schools?"

"Definitely. McGill and Concordia are there. And I always have fun when I go back. That's where I was born."

I lean my chin into my palm. "Really? So now you live here with just your mom? Or is she remarried?"

"Just my mom."

"When did you move here?" I suddenly have a lot of questions for adorable Bryan. I want to know all about him.

"After I finished grade six—or sixth grade, as they say here. When my mom and dad split, my mom decided to come here with me."

"I bet with a name like Florence, you expected this place to be a little more glamorous. Like they'd serve gelato and fresh mozzarella in the cafeteria."

He laughs. "I guess."

"Do you get to see your dad?"

He shrugs. "He's remarried now, has a new baby."

"So that's a no?"

"I go up about once a year."

I shake my head. "I can't imagine only seeing my dad once a year."

"Long distance sucks, no?"

"No?"

He laughs. "It's a Montreal thing."

Ivy does it too. I guess she got it from Bryan. I wonder what else she learned from him.

"So, do you find the long distance with Ivan tough?" he asks. "I don't think I could ever do a long-distance relationship."

"It can be difficult," I say. I don't want to talk about my imaginary boyfriend. "But I do know how it feels to miss your dad. My dad's a workaholic, so we don't spend too much time together."

"That sucks."

"Yeah. Not as much as it must have sucked to move in the sixth grade, no?"

He smiles. "It wasn't too bad. I met Jerome. He's a good guy."

"Oh! Jerome." I know I'm supposed to unfix him up with Joelle, but how do I do that when I haven't even fixed them up?

"What about him?"

I don't know how to say it without sounding weird. "Nothing. Never mind."

"Is it about Joelle?" he asks.

"No," I say firmly. "Why? What about Joelle?"

"That Jerome likes her. I think he's going to ask her out. What do you think? Is she into him?"

"No," I say quickly. "She isn't." There we go! Easy peasy!

"Oh," he says, blinking. "That's too bad."

"Yeah. She doesn't like him," I continue. "Sorry. You should tell him not to ask her out." Ivy owes me one.

"He's gonna be bummed," Bryan says with a frown.

I wave my hand. "They're not a good match." He's gonna dump her anyway. "Now back to you. If you're from

Montreal, how come you don't have an accent or any-thing?"

"My dad speaks English. I did go to French immersion when I lived up there. If you ever need help in French, I'm your man."

I straighten up. "You're helping me? I'm the one who's supposed to be helping you." I glance at my watch. We have only ten minutes left. "Should we get to work?" Not that I want to be talking American history. I'd rather be learning the history of Bryan.

"Oh, don't worry," he says. "I'm not doing that badly in American history. In fact, I don't even have Fungas."

"Really? So why did you sign up for tutoring?"

His cheeks turn red. "I wanted to spend time with the tutor."

Pop! Pop! Pop!

chapter thirty-nine

Thursday, June 5 • • • Senior Year

I'm waiting to be picked up. And waiting. And waiting some more. Where is Joelle? It's already ten to eight. I hope nothing bad happened.

I wait another five minutes and then run back inside to call her cell on my house phone. Where are they? School is going to start any second! I really need to buy a new phone. Not to replace my magical one, but to be able to communicate with people who, um, aren't me.

"Hello?" Joelle says.

"Hey! What happened to you?"

Silence.

"Joelle?" I say.

"Who is this?" she asks.

"It's me! Devi!"

"Um, hi, Devi. How are you?" Her voice sounds kind of weird. Formal.

"I'm worried! You okay? You're usually here by now."
First period is going to start any second. We have to get to
class!

I hear the school bell. She's there already? Did she just
forget to pick me up?

"Where's 'here'?" she asks.

What's going on? Why did she not pick me up? Why
does she sound so strange? Like she doesn't know why I'm
calling her.

Like we're not even friends.

Oh. My. God.

"N-never mind," I stammer. "Sorry, Joelle. I called the
wrong number." I click off the phone, stare at it for a moment, and then run upstairs to my room.

The pictures are gone. The frames are still there, but instead of shots of me, Tash, Joelle, and Karin, there are shots
of me and Celia King.

chapter forty

Thursday, September 22 • • • Freshman Year

I'm walking to the cafeteria very, very slowly. I know something is going down. I don't know what or when. But I know it's bad.

Ivy gave me an earful this morning.

"What did you do?" She was seething.

"Nothing!" I told her. I really had done nothing. After our tutoring session was over, I said good-bye to Bryan and that was it.

And anyway, I don't think what happened had anything to do with Bryan, because if it had, his pictures would have been up there, not Celia's.

"Well, you ruined everything," she huffed. "Prom's tomorrow and I have no idea who I'm going with or who's in my limo. I'm probably doubling with Celia and Bryan. Or maybe I'm their third wheel. Thanks a lot."

"But I don't even know what I did," I whimpered.

"Figure it out and fix it."

Eeeeeeep.

"I can't do everything!" I screamed, finally losing it. "I can't get straight A's and be on yearbook and tutor and be in the play and start a golf team and keep my friends! I'm tired!"

"Toughen up," she barked. "Don't be such a baby."

"Easy for you to say. You don't have to do anything," I moaned. "All you do is hang out with your friends."

"Until they're no longer speaking to me."

"You wouldn't even have friends if it weren't for me," I reminded her.

"Fix it," she snapped before hanging up.

Everyone was normal this morning. Karin, Tash, and Joelle were all hanging out by our lockers and laughing.

Nothing weird.

I had American history with Karin. We sat together. All normal.

I hate this feeling, though—that at any moment, my entire world is going to explode. I have no idea where the bomb is hidden, but I know it's somewhere and it's going to blow up in my freshman face.

I don't see my friends in the caf, which makes me nervous, so I buy a grilled cheese, chips, and juice and then head downstairs to yearbook.

Boom.

Tash, Karin, and Joelle are all huddled together outside the door, whispering.

Tash's arms are crossed, Karin looks like she's about to cry, and Joelle's eyes are flashing.

"Hi, guys," I say warily.

"We have to talk to you," Karin says, and motions me into the huddle.

"Just tell me the truth," Joelle snaps. "Do you like Jerome Cohen?"

My jaw drops. "What? No!"

"Don't lie," she says, her voice wavering.

"I don't like him! I swear!"

Joelle puts her hands on her hips. "Then when you found out he liked me, why would you tell Bryan that he shouldn't ask me out?"

Uh-oh. My stomach twists. My mouth opens again, but I don't know what to say. What reason could I possibly have?

"Bryan told Jerome, and Jerome told JT, who told Celia, who told me, so don't pretend it didn't happen."

I don't try to deny it. I can't.

"I think it's because you like him yourself," Joelle continues. "That's why you kept trying to get me to like Nick Dennings instead. And why you wouldn't go out with Bryan. That's so sick, Devi. You could have just told me you liked him. You didn't have to lie to Bryan."

My mouth is dry. She's never going to forgive me.

I look up at Karin, hoping she'll defend me, but the hurt in her eyes tells me something else. That she believes it. That she's thinking about Anthony Flare—the guy I went out with in middle school even though I knew Karin liked him.

I don't know what to tell them. I need Ivy to tell me what to do.

So I say nothing.

Joelle shakes her head. "I think I'll skip yearbook today. I'm not really in the mood." She takes off down the hall, Tash and Karin close behind.

chapter forty-one

Thursday, June 5 • • • Senior Year

"You have to tell me what to do," she says after spilling the whole sorry saga. It's after school and I'm back home in my room. Frosh is supposed to be at rehearsal, but instead, she's in the school bathroom talking to me.

Eeeeeeeep!

Sure, now she's asking for my advice. When we're almost entirely out of battery. Any minute now, the phone is going to die. There are no bars left. Zero.

I can't believe she didn't tell me right away about Bryan's weaseling his way into tutoring. What was he doing at tutoring, anyway? Bryan never went to a tutor his entire high school career. Obviously, he was just going to get close to her. To me.

"We don't have time for these kinds of screwups," I snap. I'm sitting cross-legged on my carpet, all my tests spread out on the floor around me like a blanket. "You need to focus; we're out of time."

I've tried everything. I called the manufacturer. I called the phone company. Nothing works. The phone is not charging. Our time is up.

"But what am I focusing on?" she asks, sounding panicked. "School? Friends? Staying away from Bryan?"

My heart is hammering against my chest like I've just run a marathon. "School! You have to focus on school!"

"But what about Karin and my friends?"

Eeeeeeep!

"Forget about them for now," I say hurriedly. "I need to give you the answers to all the tests I have before the phone dies."

"But what will I do?"

"You'll have to ask yourself, what would Ivy do? 'Kay? Can you do that?"

"Yes," she says.

"Good. Now don't talk, just write."

"But—"

Eeeeeeep!

"We're going to start with the big ones. Junior-year math exam. It's multiple choice, so I'm just going to read out the answers. Ready? C, B, A, D, A—"

"Wait! I'm never going to be able to remember a whole bunch of letters! I need the questions!"

"There's no time! Take the answers!"

"But I need to get something to write on."

Is she kidding me? "Hurry up!"

"I'm in the bathroom! I don't have a pen on me! I just have eyeliner!"

"Use that!"

"And what will I write on? Toilet paper?"

Eeeeeeep!

I want to bang the phone against my head. "This is why I told you to carry the notebook with you at all times! Don't you listen?"

"I'm sorry, I'm sorry—it's in my schoolbag in my locker! Please stop yelling at me! I'm doing the best I can!"

I take a deep breath. "Use the toilet paper."

"Seriously?"

"If it's your only option, then yes. I'll start again. Ready?"

"Ready."

Eeeeeeep!

"C, B, A, D . . ."

I run through the math exam, and then a chemistry exam, and then four additional midterm exams before the beeping starts coming every two seconds and we can barely hear each other.

"What about the French test tomorrow?" Frosh shouts. "Do we have time for that? I'm still a disaster in that class and I need your help."

I flip through the mess of papers on my floor. "Hold on, let me find it. Here it is, here it is! Ready? The answer to the first question is—"

Eeeeep! Eeeeep! Eeeeep!

The phone goes dead.

chapter forty-two

Thursday, September 22 • • • Freshman Year

All I hear is quiet.

Oh, no. "Hello?" I squeak. "Hello?"

"Are you talking to me?" someone on the other side of the bathroom door asks.

"No. Sorry!" I'm sitting on the closed toilet seat, a heap of scribbled-on toilet paper across my lap.

She's gone.

What am I going to do now? How do I know who to be friends with? Who to go out with? What's going to happen next? And what am I going to do about the French test?

The phone vibrates in my hand.

Yes! It's her! She's back! She's figured out how to save us! I snap on the phone. "Thank God!" I gush.

"What a nice hello," the voice says. Not Ivy's. A boy's voice. Bryan.

"Hi," I say, startled.

"Hi," he says, and I can hear his smile through the phone. "What are you up to?"

"Oh, I'm—" I look around the stall. "I'm still at school."

"Yeah? Me too. I was looking for you, but I didn't see you."

"I'm just at my locker," I lie.

"I'm at your locker."

Busted. "You got me. I'm in the bathroom."

He laughs. "What are you up to this afternoon?"

Watching my life fall apart? I wonder if he could help me with the Jerome situation. But how could I possibly explain it to him? "I'm supposed to be at play rehearsal," I say instead. "But I should really be studying for a French test I have tomorrow."

"Do you need help?" he asks. "I *am* bilingual."

"Oh, um . . ." I don't know! Would I like his help? How am I supposed to know what to do?

"Meet me in the media room," he says. "I'll help you."

"Right now?"

"Would you rather spend the rest of the afternoon in the bathroom?"

I giggle. "Nah, it's kind of stuffy in here."

Ivy did say that keeping my grades up was my number one priority. Without the answers to the test, I might get another F. And Bryan's the only person I can turn to. I can't talk to Ivy anymore, and my friends aren't speaking to me. Who else is going to help me?

"Hello? Devi? Are you coming?"

But I'm not supposed to spend time with Bryan. I fidget with the lock on the door. Then I let go. Then I stand up. Then I sit down.

I have no idea what to do.

chapter forty-three

Thursday, June 5 • • • Senior Year

Ahhh! My acceptance letter morphed the second the phone died. Harvard is gone. I've been accepted by NYU, which might be a top school, but it's not number one, and worse, it's not offering me any scholarship money.

What happened? I pace back and forth around my room. What do I do?

I can't breathe in here. It's too hot. The room feels smaller. Did it shrink? Did Devi do something to make my room shrink? I need fresh air. I grab the phone and my purse and scream to my dad that I'm taking a walk. I slam the door behind me.

I sit on my front steps and inhale a big gulp of air. What am I supposed to do now? I wring my hands.

Bryan's bright blue Jetta pulls into my driveway. My stomach twists. What's he doing here? I hug my knees into my chest.

He rolls down his window. "I've been trying to call you. Your phone still isn't working."

He's talking to me. What does that mean? Why is he talking to me?

"It's broken," I say.

"I tried to find you after class, but you bolted out of there."

"Stuff to do," I say. I don't know where to look. I don't understand what he's doing here.

"Come for a drive," he says.

Huh? "I don't know."

His forehead wrinkles in confusion. "Why not?"

I look down at my wrist. The bracelet glistens back up at me. What does this mean? What did Frosh do? Did she fall for him? Did we go out? Are we still—my heart leaps—together?

I hurry down the steps and get into his car.

chapter forty-four

Thursday, September 22 • • • Freshman Year

I'm sitting across the table from Bryan in the media room.
He's so cute. He really is.

I can't stop smiling. So I won't get an A. I can accept
that. But I'm pretty sure I won't get another F. Bryan's being
really helpful, and I'm kind of following what he's saying—
when I'm not staring at his lips.

Sweet lips.

Adorable lips.

Sure, I might not get into Harvard, but that's three years
away. Do I really have to worry about it now?

No, I do not.

Without Ivy on the other end of the phone, I don't have
to obsess about college. Or about tomorrow. Or about anything that isn't happening across the table from me.

It's time for me to make my own decisions.

"Hi," I say, smiling. I can't help it. He makes me smile.

He grins back. "Don't you mean 'bonjour'?"

chapter forty-five

Thursday, June 5 • • • Senior Year

We drive down the block, and he stops the car in front of Hedgemonds Park. Superb. The place of our first kiss.

"So your phone. It finally went to cell phone heaven?" he asks.

Instead of looking at him, I stare out the window at the swings. "I guess. It doesn't seem to be charging."

"Do you want me to take a look at it?" he asks.

"If you want to." I reach into my purse, pull out my phone, and give it to him.

Our hands touch and a spark zooms up my arm.

The next thing I know, he's leaning over and we're kissing. His lips are sweet and soft, and everything feels so right and safe. He's mine again.

It's perfect. We're perfect. Everything is the way it should be. Everything's the way it was.

He must have changed his mind. Something must have

happened to change his mind. Maybe Frosh said something or did something to make him love me enough. And now he's going to stay. He isn't going to leave me. All thoughts of college, all thoughts of friends, are long forgotten.

"I love you," I tell him.

"I love you too," he says. "You better come visit."

What? I pull back, my body suddenly cold. "You're still moving to Montreal?"

He blinks. "Yeah."

I can't breathe. It's like someone is stepping on my throat. "You're leaving me?" I whisper.

His face twitches. "I . . . yeah. We talked about this. You know I'm going to Montreal. It's what's best."

A tsunami of sadness overwhelms me. "I can't believe you're still going." I am suddenly furious with him. Furious with myself for even getting into his car. For letting him kiss me. One kiss and I forget everything I've been working for? All my plans? What about me? What about what's best for me?

He grabs hold of my shoulder. "But we agreed that breaking up was the right thing. You wanted—"

"You agreed! I didn't agree to anything!" Could I have agreed to this? Is that possible? How could I have agreed to it? What's wrong with me? Who am I? The tears are running down my cheeks now, burning my skin. I need to get out of here. This second. My hands are shaking as I grab for the handle, yank the door open, and start running home.

"Devi, wait," Bryan calls. "Let's talk about this. Please?"

Instead of answering, I keep walking.

"What about tomorrow? Can we talk about tomorrow? It's prom!"

I'm not going to prom with him. I'd rather go alone. I'd rather go with Tom. Someone who means absolutely nothing to me. Someone who will never hurt me. I grab at the clasp of the bracelet on my wrist and this time manage to get it off. For good. "Stay out of my life," I beg.

"Come on, Devi. Please talk to me."

I don't listen. I don't look back.

I should never have looked back.

chapter forty-six

I'm at my locker when I see the text from Bryan.

When is ur test?

I text back: 4th.

He writes: Gd lck. Wanna go for lnch after 2 celebr8? My bench wants to meet u.

Tee hee. I'm about to write back *YES* but my fingers hesitate over the keypad.

Ivy would not be pleased. But I like him! And anyway, why should I do what she says anymore? How do I know if she's *still* right? Things change. Just because things ended badly for her, it doesn't mean they'll end badly for me. What if Bryan doesn't cheat on me this time? He might not. That he did once doesn't mean he'd do it again.

I swallow hard. Yeah, I know, every Lifetime movie would tell me otherwise.

But this is different. I'm different.

Is it fair to punish someone for something he hasn't done yet? It's not like he cheated on *me*. He cheated on me in the future. In one version of the future. And if I've learned anything in the last two weeks, it's that there's more than one version.

Yes! I finally write back.

chapter forty-seven

Friday, June 6 • • • Senior Year

"What's wrong with you?" Celia, all glittery, is standing in front of my locker. "You better not be a misery tonight. Perk up! It's prom. And at least we get out of here at eleven! You definitely need the time to get your hair and nails done."

Ugh. Does this mean I'm in a limo with Celia? And who else? Who's my date? Am I going stag now that I told Bryan to take a hike? Is Celia going with Bryan? My head hurts.

"I have a headache," I tell her.

The truth is I'm not feeling as crappy today as I thought I would. The tears dried up by the time I got to my door, and then I just felt empty. Tired and empty.

Even though the picture of Bryan was back in its frame, even though the Harvard acceptance letter was gone, I did not cry. I'm stuck with whatever I have. If the phone battery is dead, then so are the Frosh-induced changes in my life.

So Bryan's leaving me. He doesn't need me anymore. No one needs me. The one person who did need me—Frosh—is history.

What can I do? Nothing. Absolutely nothing. And NYU is still an amazing school. So I don't have a scholarship. I can get a loan. Or I can work for a year and save up. I can figure something out. And I may not have my old friends anymore, but I can make new ones in New York.

"Dev?" I hear.

I'm startled out of my thoughts to see Bryan standing in front of my locker. What does he want? Didn't I make myself clear?

"Can we talk?" he asks. "I don't understand what happened last night. I thought we discussed—"

"I don't know what we discussed," I blurt out, clenching my jaw. I don't know anything except that I want him to go away. I want to punch him in the chest. I want to pull him toward me and kiss him like crazy.

"I fixed your phone," he says, rummaging through his bag. "The battery from the camera you bought me fit. It doesn't have much juice, but the charger will work. You can keep it if you want." He holds out my phone and a black charger.

My head spins. "The camera battery works in my phone?"

"Yeah."

How could that be? "Wait. My phone is working?"

"Yeah."

Frosh. Her French test. Today. I need to call her. Right

now. "Wow," I say, grabbing it from his hand. I still feel the sparks, but this time I pretend they don't exist.

He chews on his bottom lip. "We'll talk later, then?"

"Fine, later, whatever." I turn my back to him, ignoring his pained expression, and hit send. It's ringing. Hallelujah, it's ringing!

And ringing.

And ringing.

"Hiya, this is Devi. I'm out and about and can't take your call—"

Ahhhh! Why isn't she answering? Can't she tell how important this call is?

Now the bell is ringing. Crapola. I need to tell her what to write on the test. I call again. Voice mail again.

I'll just have to text her the answers.

chapter forty-eight

Friday, September 23 • • • Freshman Year

I'm about to close my locker before heading off to French class when I glance at my phone.

Two hang-ups, three messages, and seven texts.

The first message is Ivy screaming, "We're back on!" That explains it all.

Oh.

Yay.

I should be happy. But then why does it feel like a balloon in my chest has lost all its helium?

One of the texts is just a string of letters. B. C. D. B. A. D., and so on. Huh? I look up at the heading. FRENCH ANSWERS. Oh.

The phone vibrates in my hand, and I answer immediately. "I don't need them," I say.

Ivy laughs. "Well, hello to you too."

"Hi," I say, leaning against my locker.

"I got it working," she squeals. "It's fixed! Aren't you relieved?"

"Of course," I say, and then wonder if it's true. Yes. It must be. Who wouldn't want to speak to herself in the future? "I'm very relieved. It's just that—I don't need your answers. I studied for the test."

"No, no, no," Ivy says. "You only get a B. I checked. And you lose our acceptance to Harvard."

I kick my heel into the ground. "Because of one test? One freshman test? How does that happen?"

"Maybe it's like the SATs. You know how those first few questions are really important and determine how hard or easy the next questions are, which determines your final score? I think it's like that."

I don't respond.

"I texted you the answers. Bring your phone into class and you'll have everything there. You'll get your A. You need my help. Trust me. You need me."

"I can't bring the answers into class," I whisper. "That's *really* cheating."

"It's no worse than what we've already done. Just do it. And, Dev—whatever you're up to with Bryan? Stop it, okay?" She doesn't elaborate. She just hangs up.

I swallow hard and squeeze the phone until my knuckles turn white. I have the answers. I don't want to get a B. I want to get an A. I want to go to Harvard. I think.

I *have* to go to Harvard, or Ivy will be mad at me. I'll be mad at me. So I have no choice. Right? I slip my cell into my pencil case and close my locker. I can do this. I have to do this. It's not like I'm going to get caught. If I were, Ivy would know.

Everything will be fine from now on. Every choice I need to make, she'll tell me what to do. I square my shoulders and hug the case all the way to class. I slip into a desk at the back of the room. I open the text with the answers and then adjust my phone in my pencil case to where I can see it but Madame Ritale won't. I take out my pencil and drum it against the desk.

The student in front of me passes back the test booklet.

I glance at the answer to question number one on my cell. I fill in the letter B.

chapter forty-nine

Friday, June 6 • • • Senior Year

I'm on my way home when the world shifts. Instead of standing at the crosswalk, waiting for the light to change, I'm standing in front of racks of jeans and shirts. Where am I? Did I just get hit by a car and fall into a coma?

And why am I folding a pair of jeans?

I look around the room again. Wait. I know where I am. I'm in Bella Boutique at the mall. Why am I not on my way home to get ready for prom? Not that I know who's picking me up. Or at what time.

Maybe Frosh did something in the past that's making me come here to exchange my shoes? I glance around the room for someone to ask, but no one else is here.

"Hello?" I ask, but no one answers.

"Hello?" I repeat from the center of the store.

"Hello?" a woman with a nasal voice responds.

"Oh, good! Hello!" The voice is coming from a changing room in the back. Maybe she can tell me what's going on.

"Can you get me a size eight, please?" the nasal woman asks.

She must be talking to someone else. Not that I see anyone else. But that must be it. I'm not working today. It's not even summer. I just need to find my schoolbag.

"*Hellllo?*" the woman with the nasal voice says again. "Did you hear me? I need a size eight."

Where is my schoolbag?

The changing room door is thrown open and an older woman who's had way too much Botox slits her eyes and hollers at me, "Do you work here or not?"

Veronica, the store manager, peeks out of the staff room. "Devi, is there a problem? Can you get the customer her size?"

Oh. My. God. I am working here. And it's not even summer or winter holidays.

But why am I working on the day of my prom?

"Earth to Devi," Veronica says. "The customer would like the Dolly jeans in a size eight."

"Right. Sorry." I snap to attention. "Ma'am, the jeans are made really small. Do you want to try a bigger size?"

"No!" She scoffs.

Okay, then. My head spins as I search for the size and then pass them over the changing room door. When I turn around, I spot my reflection in the mirror.

My hair is bright pink and cropped. Plus I have a tattoo of a cell phone on my wrist.

My stomach swoops.

Where's my hair? Who am I? Did I morph into some-one else's body? What's going on? *Ahhhhh!* I need to call myself this second. My phone must be in my schoolbag. Where the heck is my schoolbag? The staff room—it must be.

I pull back the curtain. Veronica is sipping a cup of cof-fee and reading a magazine.

"Do you know where my schoolbag is?" I ask, my heart pounding.

"Why would you bring a schoolbag?" she asks.

"Didn't I come from school?"

She stares at me blankly. "School? Since when?"

Now I feel sick. "I—I dropped out?"

"That's what you told me." She flips the page of her magazine. "Didn't you hate Heken?"

My legs turn to jelly. The school for delinquents? "When did I start at Heken?"

"Wouldn't you know that better than me?"

"Yes, I should, but I have a killer headache, so can you just tell me?"

"You really need to ease up on the drinking, Dev. I bet you were out with JT again, huh?" She flips another page in her magazine. "Didn't you start at Heken after you got booted from Florence West for cheating?"

I gasp and grab on to the curtain for support. Frosh got caught. With the cell phone. And I ended up here.

I want to strangle her. How could she have screwed up so badly and gotten me into this mess? And how pathetic did I become that I'm with JT? I need my phone. Where's my phone?

"These are too small!" the customer yells. "Why would you bring me something that doesn't fit? Are you an idiot?"

"Devi, can you take care of Mrs. Arnold, please? I'm on my break."

I try to nod, but my whole body feels numb. I step out of the staff room and knock on the changing room door.

Just get through this, I tell myself. Then you'll find your phone and straighten everything out.

She throws open the door, clad only in her beige panties and red blouse. "Are you trying to make me feel fat?"

I shake my head. "I told you they ran small."

She digs her fingers into my arm. "So you think I'm fat?"

I really can't deal with this right now. I pull myself out of her grasp. "No, I do not. The jeans are made small. I wanted to get you a size ten. You wouldn't let me."

"So this is my fault?"

That's it. "Yes! It's your fault!"

"Devi!" Veronica says, pushing back the staff room curtain.

"Well, it is! It's her fault!" I shout. "It's all her fault! Her fault, her fault! Her fault!"

Veronica and the customer are gaping at me.

None of this is my fault. It's her fault. And Frosh's fault. And Bryan's fault. Hers for getting caught and Bryan's for ruining my life.

"The customer is always right," Veronica tells me under her breath.

"So does that mean I'm always wrong?" For telling Frosh to use the phone? For letting Bryan become my whole life? I know this is no longer about the customer. It's about me.

"I'm sorry," I say, my eyes filling with tears.

Veronica sighs. "Devi, I'm going to have to ask you to leave immediately."

Superb. Now I'm getting fired from a job I didn't even know I still had. I blink quickly to stop the tears from spilling over and push my way out of the store.

I need my phone. I *really* need my phone. "Devi, you forgot your purse," Veronica calls after me.

Of course! If I don't go to school, I don't have a schoolbag; I have a purse. Yes! "Thanks," I mumble, rushing back into the store and then running back out with it.

Please be in here, please be in here. I look under my wallet. No phone. In the pockets. No phone. It has to be here somewhere.

I walk over to the fountain and dump the entire contents of the purse onto the bench.

No phone. I have no phone.

Where is it? Did I leave it somewhere? Or—I'm almost knocked over with nausea—was it confiscated after I got caught?

What have I done?

I can't breathe. I need more air. I don't think I can stand anymore. Black spots are swirling in front of my eyes like smoke and I'm falling . . . and the fountain is rushing toward me.

chapter fifty

Friday, September 23 • • • Freshman Year

A new text pops up on my screen.

`Ur gonna do gr8.`

From Bryan.

My stomach lurches. I might throw up all over my test paper. I'm making myself sick.

I don't want to cheat. I don't *need* to cheat. I can do this on my own.

I don't want to break it off with Bryan either. I want to make him proud. I want to make myself proud. Instead of making myself sick.

But you need to get an A! Her voice screams in my head. Even when she's not yelling in my ear, I can hear her. *You have to get an A!*

No, I tell her. I don't.

I turn my phone off and shove it back into my pencil case.

This is my life. These are my decisions. If there's one thing she taught me, it's that she made her choices. Now it's my turn to make mine.

chapter fifty-one

Friday, June 6 ● ● ● Senior Year

I'm wet.

Soaking wet. Rushing water pounds my hair, my face, and my mouth. I'm in the fountain. Am I drowning? Did I die?

Wait. The fountain tastes like shampoo. I blink open my eyes.

I'm in a shower. My hair is full of suds.

Could it be?

It must be.

I'm in my house, in my lemon-fresh shower, getting ready for prom.

chapter fifty-two

Friday, September 23 • • • Freshman Year

I take the test. I don't ace it—far from it—but I get a whole bunch of answers right. I'm guessing I'll get a B.

Not an A, but still. I got it on my own. Well, not entirely on my own; Bryan's tutoring definitely helped.

I look everywhere around school for Bryan but don't see him. I reply to his text.

```
It went gr8! Thank you soooo much 4 ur
help. Ur the best. Can't make lunch.
Something important 2 do. Can I get a
rain check for after school?
```

After I hit send, I turn my phone off. I think I've earned a break.

I know I'm supposed to be at golf, but life is about choices, isn't it?

I spot the three of them at our table in the cafeteria and march right over.

They stop talking when they see me.

"Hi," I say, sliding into a seat. "I know you guys are mad and you have every right to be. I know I screwed up. But it's not because I like Jerome. I don't. I like Bryan."

Joelle shakes her head. "But then why—"

"I told Bryan you didn't like Jerome because I didn't think he was good enough for you. But that was wrong. I don't get to choose who you go out with. It's your decision, not mine. I'm sorry. Really sorry. Will you forgive me?"

She nods. Slowly, but she nods. "Of course. So you don't think he's good enough for me, huh?" Joelle asks. "What do you think of Kellerman? He's kind of cute."

"He is definitely cute," I say. My shoulders relax.

Tash winks at me from across the table. "He is cute," she says. "But does anyone find it odd that he's worn sweatpants every day for the last three weeks?"

"I'm sure it's just a stage," Joelle says.

Under the table, Karin grabs my hand and squeezes.

chapter fifty-three

Friday, June 6 • • • Senior Year

She finally picks up the phone at five. "Are you okay?" I ask. I'm standing in my room in my bathrobe. Since I found myself in the shower, I've known what I have to do. What I have to tell her.

"I'm fine. I just needed some time to think. Are you mad about the French test?"

I laugh. "Are you kidding me? You deserve an award!" I fill her in on what happened this afternoon—on how we almost lost everything. "You're a genius for putting that phone away, Devi. We would have been expelled."

"No way," she says softly.

Eeeeeep!

"The battery is dying again?" she asks.

"It wasn't charged all the way," I explain. "And anyway, Frosh, I've been doing some thinking too. And I"—I take a deep breath—"I think it's best for both of us if we let the battery go to battery heaven."

She pauses. "Really?"

"Yeah. I can't keep blaming you for my screwups. I have to face my, um, *our* life and that's impossible to do when I'm always looking behind me." It's a hard thing to say even though I know it's the truth. But the shock of being expelled and finding myself at Bella was too much. "And I have to give you the chance to live your life. Which *is* my life. And to make your own mistakes."

"So does that mean that you won't freak out if I want to drop some of my extracurriculars? I kind of blew off my golf meeting today. And I need to convince Tash to stay in the play without me. But I'll stick with the yearbook and tutoring. Yearbook is fun, and I think I'll be good at the teaching stuff."

"Fair enough," I say. "Although I will miss the golf skorts. Or more importantly, the bonding time with Dad. He looks so happy since he took it up again. But I guess I could ask him to hit some balls with me this weekend. Better late than never, no?"

"Sounds like fun. Maybe I'll try it out too."

"So." I take another deep breath.

"This is it?" she asks in a small voice.

I swallow the lump in my throat. "I guess it is."

"We're gonna say good-bye? Forever? That's so scary."

"It shouldn't be too bad. We're the same person. You can always talk to yourself in the shower."

She giggles. "But who am I going to rely on?"

I relied on Bryan. She relied on me. Who's left? "You should call Maya," I tell her. Yeah. Maya. Maya, who'd been right all along.

"And what should I do with the notebook? With all the advice? What about all the ways we were going to save the world?"

I open my desk drawer and see the green spiral notebook containing both our lists staring up at me.

"I think you should toss it," I tell her.

"Really?" she asks.

"Yeah. Who knows what changing them could lead to? We don't want to accidentally start a world war."

"Okay," she says.

I blink and the notebook is gone.

"Any final piece of advice?" she asks.

"Yes, actually." Now I giggle. "Remember that Dolly jeans are made small, and that they won't stretch. If you buy them, buy one size up."

Beep!

"That's my call-waiting," she says.

Goose bumps cover my arms and I know who it is. "Bryan," I say.

"Yeah." She hesitates. "He's on his way over. But I'll tell him not to come. If you don't think he should. Honestly, you *do* know him better than I do. And I know you said he's going to cheat on me, but maybe he won't this time. Isn't it possible?"

I swallow hard. "I have to tell you something. He never cheated on me. I made that up so you wouldn't go out with him. Really, we broke up because he was moving to Montreal to be with his dad, and he thought we should try being on our own." I brace myself for her reaction.

"Well, that's a relief."

"It is?" I expected her to be furious with me.

"I mean, it's not a relief that he broke up with you but I'm glad he wants to spend time with his dad. And, Ivy, well, isn't it possible that now that I'm not going to focus only on him, we may not break up?" Her voice is bursting with hope. "Maybe now that I have other stuff going on— my friends, and yearbook and tutoring—maybe our relationship will be entirely different." Now she even sounds like Maya. "Maybe it'll last," she continues. "Maybe we'll try long distance. Or who knows, maybe we'll end up at the same college together after all!"

I glance at the acceptance letter on my wall. It's still NYU. And if what Bryan told me yesterday is still true, he's still planning on moving to Montreal. And I'm going to New York City. And we're still breaking up.

I open my mouth to tell her the truth. That it's not going to work out. That they're going to break up anyway. That it's going to break her heart.

Breaking up sucks. Although talking to Bryan yesterday, well, it hurt, but it hurt less than it did two weeks ago. Maybe it's not the end of the world?

I glance at the pictures on my nightstand. The pictures of Bryan are still in their frames. But now there are more frames. Bryan onstage playing the drums. Me, Karin, Tash, and Joelle at a concert. And me and Maya at what looks like a dorm party. When did that happen? I wonder—maybe the key *is* balance. Maybe it's about living in the moment while still keeping your eye on the big picture—on all the pictures. And maybe it doesn't matter if Bryan and Frosh—if Bryan and I—break up. The relationship still played an important part in my life—in shaping who I've become.

Not Ivy, the girl I wanted to be, but Devi, the girl I am.

"So what do you think?" she asks.

Just because a relationship ends, it doesn't mean it's not worth having.

Eeeeeeep!

"Who knows?" I tell her. "Maybe this time things will be different."

The phone dies in my hand.

I sit for a few moments, feeling the warmth of the phone in my palm. Then I put it down on the table.

I'm in a bit of a daze. No more Frosh. No more Ivy. No problem—I'm ready to be Devi.

I look around to get my bearings.

Next to my acceptance is a letter from the NYU Office of Financial Aid, congratulating me on my entrance scholarship.

Cool.

Maybe I was right. Maybe this time things will be different. I'll have to wait and see.

The doorbell rings, and I get ready to face my future.

chapter fifty-four

Friday, September 23 • • • Freshman Year

The doorbell rings, and I jump up to face my present.

"I'm coming!" I yell. I take the steps two at a time and throw open the door. "Hi!"

"Hi," Bryan says. "Let's go for a walk. I bet it's one of the last nice days."

"Didn't you say that last week?"

His eyes twinkle. "I might have."

I slip on my sandals. "Want to walk to Hedgemonds Park? It's right around the corner."

"Absolutely," he says, taking my hand. "We can rank their swings."

We hold hands along the way and then run for the swings.

As soon as we get there, we both start showing off, pushing higher and higher—until my sandal flies clear across the park.

He laughs and jumps off the swing to get it.

"Sandal found!" he hollers, and holds it out toward me Cinderella-style. I slow to a halt.

"What about Ivan?" he asks.

"Ivan and I are . . . over."

He places his hands over mine, leans down, and kisses me.

His lips are soft and light and sweet, and everything else disappears except for the kiss and the moment. The perfect kiss in this perfect moment.

chapter fifty-five

Friday, June 6 • • • Senior Year

The doorbell rings and I'm not even dressed yet.

But yay! Prom people are here! Excitement flutters down my back and to my toes. I wonder who it's going to be. My friends? Tom? Harry? Bryan?

No matter who it is, I'm going to have a great night. I will take whatever comes and enjoy the moment.

Even if it's Cèlia.

But I really hope it's not her.

"Mom, Dad, can you get it?" I call. I pull on my beautiful silver dress from Raffles and my original heels. My original red heels. How about that? They look really cool with the dress. Who would have thought?

Now what jewelry should I wear?

I think of the bracelet I shoved into my purse. Even if he's not here, I know it will look just right.

Bryan is waiting for me at the bottom of the steps. I

catch my breath. He looks absolutely adorable—absolutely *dimples*—in his tux.

"Hi," he says, pulling me into a hug. "You're gorgeous."

"Thanks," I say, inhaling his scent. "You too."

"You guys both look amazing," Mom says. Meanwhile, I can't believe how amazing *she* looks. Not as glamorous as Millionaire Mom, but her hair is in a bouncy ponytail, her skin is glowing, and she's back to a size 6. "I can't believe how quickly time has passed," she continues. "It seems like just yesterday Bryan rang our doorbell and I gave him my apple brownies."

"I do love those brownies," Bryan says wistfully.

"Lucky for you I packed you guys a snack," Mom says, and hands me a box. A box that's labeled Banks's Bakery.

Huh?

"Thanks, Mrs. Banks. You're the best. Dev, everyone's already in the limo. We should go. Mrs. Banks, do you and Mr. Banks want to take some pictures outside?" He glances at his watch—the silver watch I got him for graduation. But if I never returned the watch, then how . . . ?

"Of course," Mom says. "I think he's just out back with Maxie. We were trying to keep her out of Devi's hair."

Maxie? We got a dog?

"Dad!" I holler. "We're going outside."

Bryan takes my hand and leads me out the door.

The driver is standing beside the car, wearing a suit and a black cap. Tall, dark, Italian, handsome. He looks familiar. Where do I know him from?

Oh. My. God. It's Alfonzo! Oh, no, must hide him

before my mom comes out! "Excuse me," I say. "Um, this is going to be a while. You should just sit and wait in the car. No need to stand around."

He gives me a smile and a wink before disappearing into the car.

Yeah, I know I'm done manipulating other people's lives, but no need to tempt fate.

Karin and Stevey, Tash and Nick, and Joelle spill out of the limo.

They all look amazing. Joelle's wearing the cool purple dress she made, Tash is drop-dead gorgeous in a slinky black dress, and Karin is stunning in a low-cut red taffeta number. While her nose has definitely been altered, her boobs and lips are still au naturel. Guess it's my job to make sure they stay that way.

"So, I'm officially here on my own," Joelle says, throwing her arms in the air. "I thought Kellerman was going to ask me for sure, but too late now."

Tash lets go of Nick and puts her arm around Joelle. "It's enough about Kellerman," she chides. "You broke up with him two years ago. You need to move on."

"No kidding! But you know it was the biggest mistake of my life!"

I giggle. I can't help it. I guess Tash was right. She does like being the tortured artist after all.

"Here come your dad and Maxie," Karin says, waving to the front of the house.

I turn to see my dad helping a little girl in a pink dress and high pigtails down the steps. We must be babysitting a neighbor's kid—not that I recognize her. Not that I recognize my dad either. He's beaming and tanned and wearing jeans and a T-shirt. No bathrobe in sight. Although he is wearing his Mickey Mouse slippers. I wonder what changed for him. He looks so happy. And when did my parents decide to open a bakery, anyway?

"Your little sister is adorable," Joelle tells me.

My . . . what?

chapter fifty-six

Friday, May 23 • • • Three and a half years later

"Maxie, be careful!" I say. I hold my almost-three-year-old sister tightly by the hand. She's about thirty seconds from spilling her ice cream over everything. Guess who she got her klutziness from?

"Sorry," I say into my cell. "Karin, you still there?"

I'm standing in the mall, by the circular fountain. I'd promised my parents I'd take Maxie to get a toy golf set this morning. She's obsessed. My dad's been working on her swing during his mornings with her, before his afternoons in the bakery.

Karin sighs into the phone. "I was saying that I can't believe you guys broke up! It's so depressing! I thought you two would get married for sure."

"I know," I admit. "We still love each other. It's just that we've been together for almost four years! And with him going to Montreal and me going to New York City, we think it's time to spread our wings. You know, test out life without the other."

"But why? You like life with each other!"

"I know," I say. "I just thought . . . I don't know, I thought it would be good for us. Help us grow as people. And he agreed with me eventually. But we're not breaking up this second. Only when he leaves. And I'm still planning on visiting him in Montreal."

"But you're still going to prom together?"

"Of course! I wouldn't miss prom! Are you insane?"

"Are you sure it's the right thing to do?" she asks.

"I hope it is. It feels like it is. But I don't know."

Luckily, I'm going to have a busy summer to distract me. Working at Bella, and spending as much time as possible with the girls before we all split up, packing for college, helping plan Maxie's Little Mermaid–themed birthday party in July, and then meeting Maya for a week in Italy. And Mom and Dad are even closing the bakery for a week and we're all going down to New York City to find Maya and me a two-bedroom apartment before she starts law school and I start college. We're going to be roomies!

"It sounds like you know what you're doing," Karin says. "Time will tell, I guess."

How true. I wish I could ask my college self . . . kidding! The weeks back in freshman year when I spoke to Ivy seem like forever ago. Sometimes they feel all hazy, like a dream.

"Are you almost done at the mall?" Karin asks. "We have a ton of parties to get to today. You only get one senior skip day."

"We're leaving in two minutes," I promise.

Maxie pulls at my shirt. "Devi, I can't—" Her ice cream is precariously perched on top of the cone. It is not looking safe. I watch as it starts to slip in slow motion.

"No!" I cry, and leap toward it with my hands out.

My cell phone soars into the fountain. Whoops.

I sigh. I try to reach for it but it's too far in. Crapola.

"Stay here," I warn her. I roll up my jeans, kick off my flip-flops, and climb in.

Maxie giggles hysterically.

"Funny, am I?"

"Hee-hee-hee-hee-hee-hee!" She continues giggling, her short brown pigtails bouncing from side to side.

"Here it is," I say, picking it up and wiping it against my shirt.

I hit the power button, but it doesn't work. Neither does the one, the two, the three, the four . . .

I hit send. It rings.

"Hello? Hello?" someone says.

"Hello?" I say. "Who is this?"

"It's Devi," the person says.

Omigod! It's me! I'm calling myself as a freshman! Today's the day! How could I forget!

"Fourteen-year-old Devi?" I ask disbelievingly.

"Twenty-one-year-old Devi," the girl says slowly. "Oh. My. God. I don't believe it."

It can't be. Can it? My heart leaps. "Ivy?" I ask. "Is that really you?"

"Yes!" she exclaims. "I was just thinking about you! I'm in the campus bookstore and you're not going to believe who I just—"

"Wait!" I cry. "Don't tell me anything."

Pause. "You're right. You're so right."

"I think . . . I think I dialed the wrong number."

"Yes," she says slowly. "I think you did."

And then I hang up.

Oh. My. God. That was close. I should just throw the phone back into the fountain. Get rid of it for good.

Or . . .

I slip it into my purse. You never know. I might want to talk to her one day.

Anything's possible.

Sarah Mlynowski is the author of the Magic in Manhattan series: *Bras & Broomsticks*, *Frogs & French Kisses*, *Spells & Sleeping Bags*, and *Parties & Potions*. She also coauthored *How to Be Bad* and has written several adult novels. If Sarah could talk to her younger self, she'd tell her to be nicer to her parents, to keep more diaries, and to not, under any circumstances, trim her own bangs. Originally from Montreal, Sarah's current self lives in Manhattan and can be found online at sarahm.com.